BY WAY OF PAIN

A passage into Self

BY WAY OF PAIN

A passage into Self

SUKIE COLEGRAVE

Park Street Press
R O C H E S T E R • V E R M O N T

Park Street Press
One Park Street
Rochester, Vermont 05767

Library of Congress Cataloging-in-Publication Data
Colegrave, Sukie, 1948-
     By way of pain: a passage into self / by Sukie Colegrave.
        p.   cm.
     Bibliography: p.
     ISBN 0-89281-241-9 (pbk.)
     1. Pain—Psychological aspects. 2. Suffering. 3. Self
-actualization (Psychology) 4. Pain—Psychological aspects—Case
studies. 5. Suffering—Case studies. 6. Self-actualization
(Psychology)—Case studies. I. Title.
BF515.C64 1988
155.9—dc 19   88-25422
                                                                      CIP

Printed and bound in the United States

10 9 8 7 6 5 4 3 2

Park Street Press is a division of Inner Traditions International, Ltd.

Distributed to the book trade in Canada by Book Center, Inc., Montreal, Quebec

To Bani Shorter

When a man finds that it is his destiny to suffer, he will have to accept his suffering as his task; his single and unique task. He will have to acknowledge the fact that even in suffering he is unique and alone in the universe. No one can relieve him of his suffering or suffer in his place. His unique opportunity lies in the way in which he bears his burden.

Viktor Frankl, *Man's Search for Meaning*

CONTENTS

ACKNOWLEDGMENTS

I am grateful to Anthony Blackett, Ethné Gray, Warren Kenton, Alison Roberts, and Lee Sturgeon-Day for their contributions to the book; to Bani Shorter for the same and much more, and to my daughter, Laura, for walking beside me some of the way.

But without you, Bill, this book might not have been born. Thank you.

INTRODUCTION

Perhaps no more than at other times, but possibly with greater resourcefulness, our Western cultures endorse the flight from pain. Addictions abound as new chemicals are discovered, old chemicals used in new ways, and ordinary activities necessary to our survival, such as eating and sex, abused to satisfy hungers no physical substance can assuage.

And besides physical addictions there are emotional ones: destructive relationships cemented by fear of their dissolution; religious movements offering a collective identity to smother the aloneness that is integral to individuality; positive-thinking programs designed to obliterate uncomfortable thoughts and emotions; even spiritual practices used to assist the flight from body and earth, from feeling and suffering the wounds and imperfections whose acceptance provides us with the foundations of who we are and therefore of what we can give.

Such individual attempts to anesthetize pain are supported by institutional, social, and national ones: fundamentalist religions fanatically condemn the evil in others rather than own it in themselves; racists intent on seeing inferiority in blacks rather than accepting their own darkness; and national defense policies designed to convince us that the enemy lives outside, in other people, so that we do not have to acknowledge it within, to see it lurking in the darker corners of our own soul.

In the end all addictions and other methods of avoiding pain only succeed in postponing it and replacing authentic suffering with repetitive, uncreative suffering. The alcoholic dies of cirrhosis of the liver, the racist lives in fear of those he oppresses, and the husband is suffocated by the dead marriage he is too scared to relinquish.

The task of exchanging neurotic suffering for real suffering is the domain of psychotherapy. Here the pain is listened to and explored for its possibilities as the seedbed of psychological acceptance, integration, and transformation. But unfortunately, in its attempt to meet the human condition honestly and to take responsibility for the suffering this inevitably entails, psychotherapy often loses sight of the way beyond pain, a way that is born from suffering it. It does not see that in the darkest abyss, the place where all seems lost, a gate exists, brought into being by the suffered pain, which leads to a land beyond pain, a place of serenity and playful joy which does not deny body and earth, but includes and celebrates them. This is the story which follows. It is told through the interweaving of fiction and psychological discussion so that the reader may not only understand the passages of change which characterize this healing journey, but also touch the life of some of the inner experiences of this archetypal unfolding, and feel by way of image and story some of its different qualities, which concepts alone cannot convey. Though the characters are fictional, their experiences are real, drawn from my own life and the lives of the people I have known and worked with.

The early chapters are indebted to the ideas and practice of Jungian analysis. The later ones had their inception in a dream about C. G. Jung:

The dreamer is standing on the steps of a Spanish airport with a small group of people. They are about to catch a plane home. "Jung" appears, and offers to help them in any way that he can, in particular to answer questions about psychology. Then he turns to the dreamer, and somewhat sadly refers to the last paragraph in his autobiography, Memories, Dreams, and Reflections *(New York, 1963), expressing his regret that he was unable to explore the meaning and implications of the soul experience hinted at in this final passage of his book. He indicates that he would be glad if someone could complete the psychological story that the parameters of his life prevented him from completing.*

In the passage to which the dream Jung figure referred, C. G. Jung writes:

"When Lao-tzu says: 'all are clear, I alone am clouded,' he is expressing what I now feel in advanced old age. . . . Yet there is so much that fills me: plants, animals, clouds, day and night, and the eternal in man. The more uncertain I have felt about myself, the more there has grown up in me a feeling of kinship with all things. In fact it seems to me as if that alienation which so long separated me from the world has become transferred into my own inner world, and has revealed to me an unexpected unfamiliarity with myself" (p. 359).

Once the meaning of suffering had been revealed to us, we refused to minimize or alleviate the camp's tortures by ignoring them or harboring false illusions and entertaining artificial optimism. Suffering had become a task on which we did not want to turn our backs. We had realized its hidden opportunities for achievement, the opportunities which caused the poet Rilke to write *"Wie viel ist aufzuleiden!"* (How much suffering there is to get through!). . . . There was plenty of suffering for us to get through. Therefore, it was necessary to face up to the full amount of suffering, trying to keep moments of weakness and furtive tears to a minimum. But there was no need to be ashamed of tears, for tears bore witness that a man had the greatest of courage, the courage to suffer. Only very few realized that.

Viktor Frankl, *Man's Search for Meaning*

Chapter One

INTO PAIN

It was a cold March day. The London pavements still bore remnants of the hard night frost, and now small snowflakes were dropping on the thousands of angry marchers. Sally was among them, with her five-month-old daughter, Rachael, cocooned in a baby carrier under her leather jacket. It was 1970, and she was marching for women's rights. But she might as well have been marching against racism or the Vietnam War. For she was passionately opposed to oppression of any kind, outraged by the injustices and discrimination which seemed to define advanced industrial societies. Occasionally Luke, her somewhat more sanguine husband, risked a casual humorous remark about the fervor of her political convictions and ideals, and then rapidly regretted it as he received a fierce Marxist monologue in response. His worst offense was to quote his favorite lines from Yeats's poem "The Second Coming":

> Turning and turning in the widening gyre;
> The falcon cannot hear the falconer;
> Things fall apart; the centre cannot hold;
> Mere anarchy is loosed upon the world,
> The blood dimmed tide is loosed, and everywhere
> The ceremony of innocence is drowned;
> The best lack all conviction, while the worst
> Are full of passionate intensity.

I

Irritated by his lack of support for what mattered so deeply to her, she usually became even more heated in her defense of the party line and made another attempt to persuade him to read some of her books on feminism and socialism.

But beneath her passionate convictions disquieting questions were beginning to stir. At first she had managed to dismiss them by concentrating with greater fervor on political activities. But this rarely stilled them for long, and often seemed to strengthen them. They acquired volume, insisting on being heard. "How can you give so much of your time and energy to fighting for these ideas when you don't know why you believe in them?" the voices asked. "What is the source of your convictions?" "Where do ideas and feelings come from? What are they?"

As she listened to these questions she began to sense a wisdom in their unknown source, to recognize the futility of acting without understanding her motivations. She felt her political convictions start to drain away, leaving in their place an uncomfortable hollow. "The best lack all convictions; the worst are full of passionate intensity." Yes, she acknowledged, Yeats and Luke are right.

When she had put Rachael to bed that evening she picked up a women's liberation magazine she had been reading before the march, dimly remembering having seen an advertisement for a Jungian psychotherapist. She had been briefly interested in Jung and Freud when she was sixteen and attracted by the concept of the unconscious. So now she dialed the number.

The psychotherapist lived in a suburban section of south London, an area of small semidetached houses and neat little walled-in gardens which Sally had long associated with claustrophobic, petty-minded habits and values. But since she had made the appointment and undertaken the slow drive across central London, she decided not to be deterred by outer appearances. The inside was not much better, however. The small waiting room into which she was led by the graying, soft-spoken therapist seemed to match perfectly the exterior of the house and street. It was filled with small, well-dusted, carefully chosen objects. Sally disliked objects of any kind. She regarded them either as unnecessary clutter or as things requiring energy to be kept clean. She liked casual dishevelment, houses where things seemed to fall into and out of place with no particular order. Most of all houses which demanded minimal housework. For housework of all kinds bored her. She felt it took her away from the important and interesting things, from ideas and ideals, from passion and achievement. So, as she waited on one of the small, carefully positioned chairs, she doubted once again whether this woman could help her to understand the source of her convictions.

But once she was inside the therapeutic room itself these doubts dissolved. Not because this room was any different from the one outside; it too was filled with carefully chosen, carefully tended objects. But from inside her clean, neat clothes this graying, wrinkled woman exuded a kind of peace and listening which Sally instinctively knew could only have been born from suffering and understanding. Sitting on a slightly squeaky cane chair opposite this woman and speaking of some of her reasons for making the appointment, Sally felt she was being genuinely listened to for perhaps the first time. She could feel her words being received, being heard and compassionately held. There was none of the noise and tension which usually circulated and around other people when she tried to speak, none of the turbulence as they searched for their reply before she had even concluded her sentence. This woman did not appear to be filled with agitation. And even seemed to enjoy listening to Sally speak, as though what she was saying was valuable in itself, just because she was saying it. In the presence of such gentle, quiet receiving Sally heard her own voice quieting. Her sentences came out more slowly, and occasionally she noticed answers spontaneously arising within her in response to her spoken questions.

All too soon it was over. With a small motion of her head the therapist indicated that the fifty-minute hour had ended. Sally immediately got up, anxious not to stay a minute beyond her allotted time and risk breaking the delicious spell of quiet receptivity. But she decided to return to that quiet suburban house twice a week from then on so that she could continue to quench her newly discovered thirst to be heard.

In the ensuing weeks and months she learned some of the language of Jungian psychology and was profoundly moved by the way it seemed to correspond with and elucidate many of her dreams and daily experiences. In every way she tried to be a model patient. She wrote down her dreams and even memorized them when the gentle woman suggested that speaking her dreams might be more in tune with psyche than reading them from her dream journal. But sometimes she was not sure of the "right" thing to do. And then she found herself in a state of severe anxiety which she did her best to control. One particularly hot afternoon she walked into the therapeutic room and found a tea tray laid out between the two chairs. Her therapist explained that she herself was thirsty and suggested they have a cup of tea together before beginning the work. Sally did not pause to ask herself whether she wanted tea. Instead her thoughts revolved entirely around what would be the appropriate response. Since nothing in the therapy to date had prepared her for anything as familiar as receiving a cup of tea from her therapist, she decided on a compromise answer and asked for half a cup.

Nevertheless, after eighteen months, Sally felt that she had received so much from the work—a new respect for herself as well as new understanding and interests—that she decided the time had come to end it. After all, she said to herself, she did not want to be one of those people who remains forever in therapy. She wanted to get on with her life. She was therefore surprised and saddened when her therapist did not seem to agree with her decision, telling her that instead of it being the end of the work it might be the beginning; that though Sally had learned and observed much she had, as yet, experienced little of her pain, touched little of her soul and its potential for transformation.

But having decided to leave, Sally went ahead with her decision, thanked the therapist, and walked out into the small suburban street, feeling grateful for the hours she had spent there, but also uncomfortable with her therapist's parting remarks.

It took some time before that discomfort gained sufficient strength to take her back into therapy. But eventually it did. Two and a half years later she walked into another gentle—but very different—therapeutic room, this one belonging to a quietly radiant woman. Sitting down on a large comfortable leather chair warmed by the late autumn sunlight, Sally chose, not without considerable trepidation, to turn toward her pain.

During the ensuing years, through the hours of analysis and her own thousands of private hours of reflection and psychological listening, some of the archetypal patterns of soul being and becoming gradually revealed themselves to her. . . .

Our emotional attachment to all that is creative, loving, and vital in those we meet and know feeds our psychological unfolding. Our capacity to mother, for example, is nurtured by the selfless loving of good mothering, either when we are children or by way of a later adult relationship. This experience resonates with and waters our embryonic capacity for such love, inviting it into being. But the opposite is also true: a destructive parental experience is likely, without any later opportunity for healing, to invite another destructive parent into the world. And so our sins as well as our gifts are passed down from generation to generation.

About a year after choosing to listen to her own pain, Sally found herself also wanting to listen to the pain of others; to learn more about the nature of psychological wounding and healing. So she became a regular observer on a psychiatric ward of a large urban hospital; and here, one wet spring morning, she received a potent reminder of the inheritance of pain. She was taken to visit a recent arrival, a man who had committed many brutal and violent acts.

Alone with him, she sat silently for a moment, initially alarmed by the hatred he exuded. But soon her interest in him quieted her fear, and she asked him about his childhood. At first he seemed uninterested in talking. So they sat in silence for a while longer. But then, quite suddenly, he began to speak about how his father used to beat him for no apparent reason and then lock him in his bedroom for days, often without food. And since he had no way of knowing when this violence would occur, he explained that he lived in continual terror, simultaneously hating and fearing his father.

Momentarily shocked by his story, Sally said nothing but looked at him, feeling the connection always created between people by the speaking of truth. Then she asked him whether his father had ever talked about his own childhood.

"Yes, once. He told me his father used to beat him and then lock him in his room. He said he hated his father."

"Your father must have had a very unhappy childhood, and grown up to be a very unhappy man," Sally commented.

The man looked at her for the first time since she had entered the hospital room. Some of the anger and hate seemed to have left him, and small tears were forming at the corners of his eyes, testifying to the same pain that his brutal treatment of others had been an unconscious attempt to erase.

Sally left his room recalling the image of Rachael as she had left her that morning, sitting in her high chair beside the gentle Japanese au pair girl, her delicate infant's mouth smudged with the breakfast cereal which was absorbing most of her attention and her eyes, for a moment, reflecting the intuitive knowledge that Sally was not abandoning her by walking out the door. Standing now outside a very different door, feeling the harshness with which it was being shut and locked by the psychiatric nurse, Sally sent out a silent plea to the benevolent powers of the universe that she might avoid handing down to Rachael her own untended and unhealed wounds, that her mothering might allow Rachael to grow up with a sufficient sense of her own value to be able to foster this in her children.

The process of nourishing a child's future ability to mother or father creates a certain dependence between adult and child. For though a loving mother will help to awaken a similar capacity in her child, this child may continue to turn to the outer mother for his own mothering needs, just as the mother may spontaneously turn to her child when hungry for the innocence and vitality and the experience of becoming that are characteristic of childhood. In so doing both parent and child continue to find essential human qualities and attributes by way of each other, their psychological needs and gifts locking them into interdependence and thereby limiting their capacity to see and relate with love and understanding for who they both are, rather than for who they need each other to be.

Some dependent relationships, not just between parent and child but also between husband and wife, seem to continue reasonably harmoniously. But more often, at some moment, one of the partners in such relationships ceases to want or to be able to offer his or her side of the unconscious bargain. When this happens pain ensues. For psychological pain reflects the fact that the other onto whom an integral aspect of our being is projected has ceased, for whatever reason, either to be available to us or to live in conformity to our projection. By reflecting our loss such pain also contains the possibility of awakening us to those attributes of ourselves which we were relying on another to provide.

It was not just because he was a composer that Sally was initially attracted to Luke. She liked his refined, symmetrical features, his generous mouth, his sensitivity, and, in particular, his reserve—a mysterious mixture of shyness and consideration. But she did not fall in love with any of these qualities. She fell in love with Luke the composer.

Even though, by the time they met, his musical writing was not going well, Sally was still able to imagine his potential for writing great music, for making a significant contribution to musical history.

But soon after their relationship began it became apparent even to her that his commitment to music was diminishing rather than flowering. At first she redoubled her attempts to encourage him to start a new symphony. When this did not work, she became increasingly critical and angry with him over many seemingly unconnected details in their relating, unaware that what was really angering her was his unwillingness to carry her own unlived and still unconscious creative impulses.

When there has been no projection, loss is still experienced, but it is not accompanied by emotional pain. If, for example, a woman has discovered a conscious relationship to her psychological husband—that is, her inner masculinity—and has connected with her own wholeness, the death or departure of her physical husband will be painful only to the extent that she has enjoyed a vital, loving, and creative relationship with him. She will feel no emotional anguish, no sense of a part of her being having been torn out, since her inner equilibrium and sense of well-being will remain intact, independent of his presence. For wherever her husband may be, dead or alive, such a woman will continue to have access to her inner masculinity.

Similarly, if we are wounded by a critical comment, the pain reflects the fact that some part of our sense of self-worth is projected onto another, that we depend on the other's validation of us to feel valuable. The same critical comment might also serve to awaken us to our own critical personalities, those parts of us that judge, undermine, and condemn ourselves and others. In responding to such a comment with anger or hate we emotionally armor ourselves against the pain. For while angry and hate-filled we are unable to experience our own wounded self-worth and also unable to recognize and experience the possibilities for self-knowledge and unfolding inherent in all pain—unfree to explore the possibility that the object of our hate might be an ugly and unacceptable part of us rather than another person.

The presence of hate or defensive anger (not the righteous anger exemplified by Christ when he yelled at the merchants in the temple) always indicates an opportunity to listen inward for the true pain, to move into the wounds and often ugly inner figures which inhabit the remoter areas of soul, whose denial or unconscious repression only leaves them space to come to us by way of outer people and situations.

But even if we do not react with hate or anger at the reflections in others of our own ugliness and sickness, we may turn away in fear. The appearance of fear offers us the choice of flight from or encounter with the object of fear. When we choose flight we become the victims of the unknown beast lurking in the dark woods of our unconscious, compelled into emotions and actions by the fear of encountering it. To choose to move toward the fear, to enter the dark woods of our being and search out the beast, look into his eyes and risk feeling and suffering his beastliness, might seem foolish, even masochistic. For hunting the inner beasts obviously involves the risk of being slaughtered by them. However, a person strong enough to hunt the hunter, to turn toward the fear rather than flee from it, is usually strong enough to experience the psychic pain of the encounter without being devoured by it, strong enough to survive meeting the most ferocious beasts, mass murderers, Nazi torturers, or any other of the many destructive elements which inhabit our neglected souls, and strong enough to suffer the meeting, to receive the pain and feel the shame so fully that these inner figures can never again compel us, out of fear, into defensive and hostile feelings, thoughts, or actions.

Such strength is not born from aggression against our wounds but from consciously chosen receptivity toward them. It is a Gandhi-like strength which allows us to actively turn toward the enemy and quietly hear and feel all the anger, criticism, and hate these inner figures contain. It is the way of nonviolent confrontation in which consciousness imaginatively receives all the inner enemy has to give—each attack, each violent word, each cruel laugh, each claw or bloody tooth—until the worst is known and suffered and the ugly wound or inner figure, in becoming admitted into the light and unconditional acceptance of consciousness, is deprived of the life-sustaining energy provided for it by our fear and hostility. As this happens, the psychic energy previously locked in festering wounds and ugly psychic personalities dissolves, enabling new and creative psychic configurations to emerge. Both beast and individual consciousness are changed by their encounter with each other. Soul is cleansed and expanded, healed and transformed.

To illustrate her comments about turning toward the dark and ugly areas of soul, Sally's therapist told her the story of Beauty and the Beast. She did not tell it as a teacher of English literature might, merely summarizing the essential plot. She spoke it as she might to a child, slowly and deliberately, entering with her voice and feelings into the mood of each image. Initially Sally felt some irritation that her therapist should be speaking to her as if she were a child. She thought it a waste of expensive time. But as the story progressed these resistances diminished and she found herself being drawn into the quality of the images, drinking them in with the kind of attention which she had forgotten was possible. By the time her therapist stopped speaking, Sally felt she had been nourished not only by the psychological message of the story but also by the tone and quality of the images themselves.

Beauty's kind and gentle father asked her and her two elder sisters what they would like him to bring back from his journey. The eldest daughters, still resenting their recent decline in fortune, asked for new clothes and jewels. The merchant's favorite daughter, Beauty, said that she didn't need anything but that if her father insisted on bringing her something, she would like a white rose.

The eldest daughters' desires were relatively simple to satisfy, but Beauty's wish was not. A white rose was nowhere to be seen. So reluctantly her father started home without it. That night he lost his way in a large forest. After wandering, tired and hungry, for many hours he found himself at an old castle. Hoping for a place to rest, he tied up his horse and walked into the castle. Inside the hall he found a table laden with delicious food. Too hungry to wonder who the feast was intended for, the merchant sat down to a sumptuous meal. After dinner, feeling full and sleepy, he climbed the stairs and slept in the first bedroom he entered.

When he awoke in the morning he saw a suit of new clothes on the chair beside his bed. And downstairs he found the same table newly laid with a generous breakfast. After eating his fill, the merchant collected his horse and prepared to leave the castle. But just before he went out of the gates he saw a bush of white roses. Remembering Beauty's request, he picked one.

"Who are you?" A voice growled behind him. The merchant looked around into the eyes of a huge and ugly beast, who told him that he would be kept a prisoner in the castle unless he promised to give the Beast the first thing he saw when he reached home. Imagining it would be his small dog, the merchant agreed to the bargain.

But it was not the dog who came running out of the cottage at the sound of the horse's returning steps. It was his daughter Beauty. One look at her father's face told her that something was terribly wrong. When she heard about his promise to the Beast she insisted that it should be honored. And the next morning, filled with dread, she set off for the Beast's castle.

She expected to be greeted by the huge monster her father had described. But instead she found only the table laden with food and a bedroom containing everything she might need. That night she ate and slept little, too fearful of the Beast. But the next day, when there was still no sign of the Beast, she began to enjoy the food and the wealth of delights which had been mysteriously provided for her. And so it went on until slowly Beauty's fear of the Beast subsided a little and, in her loneliness, she found a certain curiosity arising within her about her absent host.

One evening, as she was finishing another exquisite dinner, the door opened quietly and in walked the Beast. Though he greeted her in gentle tones, Beauty was too shocked and frightened by his great ugliness to respond. Seeing her fear, the Beast retreated. But the next night at exactly the same hour he appeared again. Still Beauty was dumb with terror. But after many nights of these silent visits she found the courage to look at the Beast, even to talk to him.

During the following weeks and months Beauty's fear of the Beast faded, and she began to trust and appreciate the gentleness behind his fierce and ugly appearance. She found herself looking forward to his evening visits, even longing for them.

One evening she asked the Beast why he always looked so sad. He replied, "I love you very much, Beauty, and I would like you to be my wife."

"Oh Beast," said Beauty, "in these months I have grown to know and appreciate your gentleness, your kindness and dignity. I have even grown to love you, but I could never marry you."

The Beast sighed a deep sigh and looked sadder than Beauty had ever seen him.

That night Beauty dreamed that her father was sick and needed her. So the next evening she asked the Beast if she could return home to look after her father. Reluctantly the Beast agreed and gave her a ring, explaining that if she ever wanted to come back to the castle she had only to hold the ring and wish to return.

Beauty's father was delighted to see her alive and happy, and soon regained his health. Together they enjoyed many happy days. But one night Beauty dreamed that the Beast was dying. She saw him lying on the ground beneath the white rosebush. In the morning she told her father of her dream and explained that she needed to return to the castle.

The instant she touched the ring and wished she found herself standing beside the dying Beast. Moved with love for him, she knelt down beside his failing body and kissed his ugly head. "Oh Beast," she said "when you asked me to marry you I had to say no, because though I loved you, I was still repelled by your ugliness. But this repulsion has vanished now. I love you and want to be your wife."

Immediately the Beast rose from the ground and Beauty found herself in the arms of a noble and handsome prince. He explained to her that a wicked witch had compelled him to live as an ugly beast until such time that a beautiful girl agreed to marry him.

It was not enough for Beauty to feel compassion for the Beast. It was not even enough for her to love him. His transformation, like the transformation of all our inner beasts, required unconditional acceptance, the willingness to unite with his beastliness, to embrace all of his ugliness. Without such complete acceptance, our beasts and the other neglected and dissociated parts of us are condemned to reflect their primitive and sometimes ugly and cruel natures in our feelings, thoughts, and actions, deprived of the transforming light of the spirit which can only reach them by way of conscious acknowledgment. And inasmuch as our beasts are denied access to consciousness we are denied access to the raw, vital, and instinctual energy that is often locked within their beastly forms.

Only when Beauty was willing to marry her Beast was he able to realize his true stature, she to enjoy a man-woman relationship to him as distinct from a maternal one, and her father (whom they invited to live with them in the castle) free to exchange his impoverished state, his psychological depletion, for new wealth and vitality. Psychologically, therefore, Beauty's acceptance of her own inner beast enabled the redemption and transformation of her own masculinity and her own marriage with this inner husband. And this loving and creative act brought her psychological renewal: her father's poverty, symbolizing an outworn psychological order, was replaced by new wealth within the castle of soul.

Once the necessary courage, receptivity, and understanding are available to consciousness, withdrawing our negative projections on others by meeting, allowing, and suffering the ugly, unwanted, diseased, deprived, and hungry parts of ourselves, is often significantly simpler than withdrawing positive projections.

The most intense positive projections are often those which catapult us into love. Such experiences, sometimes lasting only a few seconds, sometimes a lifetime, tell us that we have touched a dimension of our own wholeness, united with an aspect of our inner masculinity or femininity by way of another person. At these moments we literally fall into love, join the being of love itself. Sadly, however, falling in love, while providing essential nourishment and inspiration for our own becoming, for the realization of a wholeness which is not dependent for its existence on the feelings and actions of another, does not necessarily make us more loving. It may at times make us less so. For the love of another, as distinct from the romance of being in love, depends on our willingness to take responsibility for our own emotions rather than to expect others to satisfy or alleviate them; it depends on our capacity to recognize, for example, that since emotions have their source in projection, an unrequited passion is ours to suffer and to be enriched by rather than another's to requite.

Unfortunately, the gifts and possibilities inherent in the experience of falling in love are usually lost before they are realized. The lover begins to see that the beloved does not match the ideal image, is not what she or he first appeared to be. And when this happens, the in-love experience withers as quickly as it blossomed.

The moment Sally opened the front door and saw him standing there, slightly damp in the morning mist, she knew she would rent him the top room she had decided to let while Luke was away. For his tall, angular dignity with the distant eyes and thick blackish hair stirred an unfamiliar longing. She had sometimes wondered why it was that the men she had loved, including the one she had married, had rarely been those whose bodies approximated her ideals of masculine beauty. None, it seemed, had offered her anything even approaching the elegant nobility now standing on her doorstep.

For a few weeks they lived together according to their respective roles of tenant and landlady. He developed a warm and playful relationship with Rachael, thereby relieving Sally of much of her task as Rachael's playmate when her kindergarten friends were unavailable. She would listen to the two of them rampaging and laughing together on the floor above her as she sat at her desk writing university essays. But even in those early weeks it was clear to her that they would be lovers.

When it happened she fell deeply and obsessively in love, and they enjoyed a delightful month together until one Friday evening. Sally was giving Rachael supper as he walked into the kitchen, hugged her warmly and slid himself onto the bench between the old oak table and the wall. As she cut up Rachael's food and refilled her mug with milk, she savored the thought of their time together after Rachael was asleep. She looked at him, wondering whether he had similar imaginations and longings. But in his place she saw for an instant two images. One was her lodger, a fairly good-looking, tall man with a slightly crooked mouth she had never noticed before.

And the other, unconnected to a human body, was the tall, dignified, and noble beauty she had seen on her doorstep and fallen in love with. Turning back to the human being she realized with sadness that, though she still liked him, she no longer wished to be his lover.

Occasionally the ideal image and the person who constellates it remain linked. This can occur with projections onto genuinely saintly people and also onto people removed from the lover's vision by time or space, like celluloid or fictional figures, so that the ordinary imperfections of everyday existence do not have a chance to shatter the ideal image of the projection.

Dante's fleeting vision of the fourteen-year-old Beatrice was sufficient to inspire him to travel the long and painful way to paradise. Instead of bewailing the fact that he could not love her in earthly terms, he allowed the love her image awoke in his soul to take him to the psychological place wherein he could unite with "her" for eternity. By treasuring his love for her, he allowed himself to meet and suffer all those qualities within himself which blocked or obscured a union with his image of the supreme beauty, grace, and purity of the feminine. He did not allow anger, frustration, denial, or even the numbness of passing time to dim the image of his love, but let it flourish within his soul until it became his soul.

But arduous though it was, Dante's task was relatively simple compared to that of treasuring the image of the beloved when the union has been realized in the physical world, and then, for whatever reason, ruptured. In these painful moments it is tempting to muffle the wrenching, hollow agony with one of the legion of painkillers available on this earth—drugs, alcohol, other relationships, cold intellectual disdain . . . anything that will effectively render us unconscious of the loss. Yet it is precisely this experience of loss which offers the opportunity to recognize the beloved as an integral part of our being and to begin to look for her or him within.

The search for the inner Apollo or Artemis, the Nastasia Kinski or Robert Redford entails concentrated imaginative listening; identifying and amplifying the image of the beloved until it is strong and clear enough to become a constant companion; until we can truly unite with it in love. Suffering the loss of a physical experience can assist this process of inner listening inasmuch as our souls are sensitized and strengthened by authentic mourning. Moreover, the psychic vacuum brought to consciousness by the loss is the same psychic hole which, if not filled with something else, some new projection, serves as the womb of a psychic fulfillment, becoming the vessel in which the eternal beloved is conceived and brought to birth.

Every positive projection, every image or person we admire and desire can be found within us if we honor our yearnings, relinquish and suffer their differentiation from physical forms and other people, and embrace the psychological qualities born from such sacrifice. But there is one projection which seems to belong to a different category from all others. It is the ultimate and original projection of oneness. Sometimes an "in-love" experience will reflect both kinds— the projection of certain admired qualities, certain components of our inner masculinity or femininity, as well as the projection of our psychic unity, God as well as Apollo. As the Apollo projection is withdrawn and we find our inner Apollo, we are exalted and en- nobled, purified and enlightened. As the God- or Self-projection is withdrawn and the love we found by way of another realized as the core of who we are, we find unshakable serenity and bliss, an immortality and boundlessness. A Self-projection may inspire us to undertake our own journey of becoming, to suffer its agony, to listen to its truth; it may accompany us each difficult and joyous step of the way, never dissolving until we, like Dante, reach the gates of paradise, the kingdom of heaven that is each of us.

Sally was only eighteen when she met Luke, and psychologically considerably younger. For the first year or so of their relationship he did not seem very interested in her. She felt a casualness in the way he tended to wait until about six o'clock before calling to invite her out to dinner. The early parts of many of her evenings seemed to be spent either with a dull ache inside as each hour passed without him calling, or frantically rushing to make herself as attractive as possible in the few minutes he offered her between his telephone call and his ring at the doorbell of her parents' flat.

But in the second summer of their relationship they drove across France together into Spain. And one night in a small, scruffy hotel, just across the Spanish border, as they were lying on a narrow hard bed which the hotel manager insisted on calling a double, she noticed him looking at her differently, more tenderly than usual. Then, somewhat shyly, he said, "I love you."

When they returned to London she moved into his flat and for the next year until they were married, she slept with him in his small single bed. Each night, after making love, they would mold their bodies together, fitting into each other's curves in what they called the "spoon position," and fall asleep.

The next thing she usually experienced was the harsh sound of his alarm and him leaping forcefully out of bed. Not because he welcomed the day, but because he always set his alarm for the last possible moment, just allowing himself time to wash and snatch a cup of instant coffee and a cigarette before joining the rest of those battling with London traffic to get to their offices by nine.

And every morning when he leaped out of bed in this way, harshly dismantling their "spoon" union, Sally felt he was ripping out part of her insides and taking them with him. In place of the warm fulfillment, the loving wholeness of the night, she felt herself catapulted into the day with little more than a ruptured heart.

Chapter Two

IMAGES OF SOUL

While emotions such as desire, hate, irritation, and fear indicate that an aspect of ourselves, a wound or unknown attribute, are being reflected back to us by way of another person, it is often difficult to identify the nature of these psychic components, to communicate with the unconscious aspects of our being, without the assistance of a soul language. Images are such a language. For image is born, like psyche, from the meeting of the physical and spiritual worlds, the forms of matter and the formlessness of idea.

One of the most common and useful ways in which to experience this language is in dreams. There are many different kinds of dreams, reflecting different levels, qualities, and attributes of our being and dressed in the forms of known and unknown people, animals, things, and events. Some dreams speak of the soul's impact on the body, like the dream in which the dreamer watched his shirt collar size changing from 14 to 22. Disturbed by the image when he awoke, he went for a check-up and discovered he had a malignant tumor of the thyroid gland.

Sometimes this kind of dream goes a step further by providing therapeutic insights as well as diagnosis. For instance, a woman who had recently had an abnormal pap smear dreamed of two cancer scales. One scale revealed her condition as normal, while the other, labeled as the "cold to hot" scale and associated with the mother, showed her condition to be near the far end of the cold, abnormal side. A few nights later the same woman dreamed that the cure for her cervical condition depended on clearing away the overgrown underbrush on a section of land which had once been cultivated but which in recent years had been neglected and allowed to return to wilderness.

The woman's first dream clearly indicated that her precancerous condition was associated in some way with her relationship to her mother; that an aspect of her inner mother had been left out in the cold, unintegrated into consciousness, and that this dissociated psychic content was now living and expressing itself in her body as dissociated cells—cells which, unable to respond to the totality of her organism, severed from its order, were now proliferating in chaotic and potentially destructive ways. The second dream, that about clearing the underbrush, suggested that cervical healing depended on the dreamer's capacity to return the area of her psyche, hitherto abandoned as wilderness, to a condition of cultivation; to consciously reconnect with the rejected aspects of her inner mother so that this energy could once again find its place within the order of her soul.

Most dreams of sickness, however, do not reflect a physical sickness, or at least not one which has developed sufficiently to create discernable physical symptoms. Instead they speak of psychic disturbances requiring psychic healing. Such was the case with a shocking dream Sally had soon after entering analysis.

She was with a group of childhood friends and their parents on a meticulously manicured lawn in front of a meticulously painted house. The grass had been mowed to the smoothness of a billiard table and then painted, so that it looked more like an oriental carpet than a part of nature. Even the trees and flower beds had been painted and decorated so that they appeared virtually indistinguishable from the inside of the house. The owner of the house told the guests that her daughter, one of Sally's childhood friends, was dying of cholera in an upstairs bedroom and wanted Sally to visit her.

Climbing the stairs with trepidation, Sally looked through the door into the sick girl's bedroom. Inside was a hellish melange of agony and squalor—cries of pain and death amid uncontainable layers of vomit, shit, and blood, creating a shocking contrast to the meticulously manicured house and garden.

The dream reflected Sally as having created for herself an excessively ordered and lifeless persona with which to relate to the world, masking both from it and from herself the horror and pain within her soul. The immediate task of her analysis was therefore to allow this sickness into consciousness: to accept, feel, and suffer it so that her soul, released from the straitjacket of an artificial order, could be allowed to renew and heal itself, instead of being starved of vitality by the manipulations of an ego consciousness too frightened of its own instincts to relinquish control over them.

The dream horrified and humbled Sally. It was the first time she had seen the turmoil, anger, pain, and sickness behind her carefully manicured mask. It also frightened her. Not just because of the unsuffered pain of thirty years, but because of her terror of relinquishing control, of letting go of her conscious organization of her personality.

She imagined that to stop controlling who she was—to stop sculpturing her body and soul into something more or less socially acceptable—would be to condemn herself to eternal loneliness, rejected as weird and unpleasant by all who knew her. For her controlling habits and attitudes had not only protected her from feeling her own sickness, they had also protected her from discovering and accepting who she was, an individuality she had always dimly imagined to be so unacceptable to others that it was prudent to keep it hidden.

She had begun to manicure her psychological garden as a young child. She remembered how she used to rehearse her words throughout the day if there was something she wanted to ask her father in the evening when he returned from work. And how, even after all the rehearsals, her heart would still pound with fear when she heard his car crunching over the loose gravel driveway. And he was not a cruel man. She knew that; just somewhat cold and fierce at times—unpredictable times. Nor was he the only one who frightened her. Almost everyone did, unless they were clearly her "inferior," like the family's gentle Swiss cook, to whose small stuffy room she would often escape from her fears to watch television or play cards.

Answering the telephone was a particularly alarming childhood experience. For, not knowing who it might be, she had no time to prepare something acceptable to say. Often she could avoid the experience by pretending not to hear the ringing or by waiting until someone else answered it. But occasionally it was unavoidable, and then her hands sweated as she lifted the receiver.

As she grew older her fears of the telephone, of her father, of strangers and even acquaintances diminished a little, though not significantly. But her ways of dealing with these fears improved. She discovered that asking questions used up the time in which she might otherwise have to answer them. She spent much effort on her appearance, using her manicured body as an irreproachable mask to present to the world, something whose beauty gave her some power to counteract the power she gave to others by her fear of them. More and more she used her sexuality to charm and to bewitch whenever she found herself in a threatening situation. And, for moments when this would not suffice, she trained her intellect into the services of her defense, making clever remarks to fend off potentially threatening encounters.

Such devices consumed a great deal of her energy and were not foolproof. Sometimes, nevertheless, her psychological wounds crept to the surface of her consciousness. Not frequently, but sufficiently often to enforce her fear of their pain. These moments would prompt her to redouble her efforts at control.

As she reflected now on how she had lived her life, on the constant defenses against her self and against the world, she realized how she had only been able to live like that by virtue of her blindness. Her innocence concerning the nature of and motivations for her actions had enabled her to continue to paint the grass and remain deaf to the dying cries of the young girl within her soul. But now she had dreamed the dream, and she had remembered it. She was no longer innocent. She had seen.

Though her first impulse was still to turn around, to give up the whole psychotherapeutic venture and increase her attempts to perfect the exterior of her house, she found she was unable to forget the agonized screams of the dying girl. The dream had destroyed the possibility of returning to the manicured life. She could try to walk downstairs, leaving the girl to die alone. But she knew that even if her compassion was not strong enough to turn her steps, eventually her shame would turn them. For she knew now she would never be able to wholly eradicate from her conscience the knowledge that the manicured life was just a front, an elegant escape from the untended suffering within. Though she could postpone the collapse of her defensive facade, delay the moment of relinquishing control, she realized that ultimately she could not avoid it.

Sometimes it is difficult to know which level of being—physical, emotional, or spiritual—is reflected by a dream's images, and whether it has an essentially subjective or objective meaning. As Sally began listening to her dreams she tended to regard them literally and objectively, seeing the dream characters as other and outer, having little to do with her. But slowly her analyst's sensitivity to psychological language helped her to feel her way into the images, to distinguish between those reflecting the substance of her soul, and those primarily concerned with other people and events.

Objective dreams can be prophetic or telepathic. The words and images of these are often relatively clear and direct. Sometimes they take the form of direct messages from an unknown but convincing voice, like one woman's prophetic dream in which she was told that if she went to the penthouse suite of a certain large psychiatric hospital she would find a job. The woman had been looking for experience working in a psychiatric hospital for some time, but nothing had come up. The day after the dream she met an acquaintance at a party who suggested she contact the head of a large psychiatric hospital in the East End of London. Remembering her dream, the woman acted on the suggestion and was offered a job.

Telepathic dreams often inform us of events before we have physical knowledge of them, like the dream in which a student was told of her math exam grade two weeks before she received the written result. Or a woman's dream that her immigrant visa application had been approved five days before she received official confirmation of this.

Other dreams seem to speak of events occurring in realms beyond the earth. They reflect meetings with dead people and other psychic and spiritual entities. Distinguishing between these dreams and those which reflect qualities within our own soul can be extremely difficult. It requires a sensitivity to the quality of dreams and images which only develops through long exposure to this language. If, for instance, a person dreams of a wise, spiritual being, it can be hard to know whether this being is a hitherto unconscious aspect of the person's soul or an actual spiritual entity with a relatively independent existence. From one perspective it does not matter what the answer is. The psychological priority is that the dreamer familiarize herself with and absorb the qualities of this being so that they become freely accessible to her during her earth life. For whether it is an unintegrated aspect of the dreamer or an independent entity, the dreamer's soul will be expanded by the process of integration, enriched and transformed by the new energy. If instead the dreamer facilitates a relationship to the being but insists that the image is something other or outer, though he may have access to its wisdom and gifts his soul will remain essentially confined within old boundaries. He will have acquired a friend but not an additional psychic or spiritual limb. However, once a dream has been fully milked of its subjective gifts, it is an act of respect and humility to allow for the possibility that the dream figures might also have an objective reality, that the dead husband in the dream, for example, might have something important to communicate, quite apart from enabling us to take another step toward integrating our own inner husband.

Faced with the often puzzling images of dreams, one may be tempted to explain them within the limits of one's own conceptual framework, thereby critically reducing the significance of the dream in the interest of an intelligible interpretation. The following dream analysis was provided by a spirit entity called Oracle, speaking through a trance-medium, Dr. Bernard Schechter.* Its far-reaching message may perhaps illustrate some of the dimensions of experience and understanding available to us while we sleep, as well as encourage us to live with the possibility that our dreams may contain dimensions of meaning far beyond our present capacity for comprehension.

A few days before the channeling session, Dr. Schechter dreamed of a melody sung by the pop singer Neil Diamond. But the words of the song were different. This dream song was entitled "Memphis" and was accompanied by a flash of lightning and a voice saying that "the lightning is pointing to Memphis."

Oracle explained to the audience that approximately twelve thousand years ago a city existed in the area where today the Great Sphinx and the pyramids of Gizeh stand. This city, founded by descendents of those who emigrated from the prehistorical civilization of Lemuria, was known as the holy city of Mem. The archaeological remains of the original city, according to Oracle, still exist beneath the pyramids and the Sphinx and could be discovered today if the area deep beneath these sites were excavated.

The subterranean city of Mem was built by people with advanced technical abilities in order to protect their spiritual pursuits from interference by those living on the earth's surface. According to Oracle, a portion of Dr. Schechter's soul existed (or exists in the

---

*I am grateful to Dr. Schechter for his permission to use this material.

dimension of consciousness which transcends time) as an individual in Mem and functioned in the temple of Rama. Inside this temple there existed a thin metal disc, approximately one-quarter of an inch thick and twenty-four feet in diameter. Its purpose was to produce a sound by way of the manipulation of energy patterns of the temple priests. This was done weekly to induce a trancelike state among those who tuned into it to assist their process of inner reflection.

The original emigrants from Lemuria brought with them to Mem a number of small crystals which were placed in a shootlike structure extending to the surface of the earth, through which the direct rays of the sun could at certain times pierce the crystals at such an angle so as to set off a series of intense vibrations. The vibrations passed from one crystal to the other, until their solar energy activated the metal disc and produced a different sound from that generated by the priests' own manipulations of energy.

Twice a year, at the solstice and equinox, certain angulations of the sun passing through the crystals resulted in a sound wave emanating from the disc which enabled the priests to harmonize their own energy vibrations with those emanating from the disc. This sound awakened them to a deeper experience of themselves and their interrelationships with the universe.

According to Oracle, Dr. Schechter's dream reflected that he had been spending certain sleep periods in Mem relating to a different portion of his soul and a group of other individuals. His waking memory of this experience was translated into images drawn from his earth experience. Thus the sound emanating from the sacred crystals was associated with the pop singer Neil Diamond, and the city of Mem with Memphis. The image of lightning was the dreamer's way of reflecting the concentration of solar energy being harmonized with the crystal structures in the city of Mem.

It seems likely that at least two kinds of psychological language may compose a dream: the genuine symbol such as the cat whose image expresses the psychic cat, (that part of our instinctual being which corresponds to and psychically reflects the physical cat as well as the archetypal cat), and images drawn from the nearest earth approximation of nonearthly or unknown earthly phenomena.

Some of the more readily intelligible dreams, perhaps, are those which offer the psychic underpinnings of a conscious situation; which paint an event or emotional experience in the colors and forms with which it was perceived by the dreamer's unconscious. It often happens, for example, that following an uncomfortable encounter with someone in which considerable emotion has been activated within us, we dream of someone from our past. Initially any connection between the two people seems unlikely, but as the feeling of the dream is listened to, it becomes clear that the emotion which erupted during the waking encounter really belongs, in its intensity, to our relationship with the person reflected in the dream; that it has its source in an early wound whose raw, unhealed nature was brought to consciousness by a situation bearing some resemblance to the early trauma. Once this wound is recognized and consciously suffered, the projection onto the outer figures falls away, and although a similar situation in the future might be difficult, unpleasant, or inconvenient, it will not activate the same emotional storm within us. For emotional storms are always ours. Outer situations merely facilitate their upsurge into consciousness from buried layers of our soul.

Understanding a dream evokes a "yes" from the feelings as well as the thoughts of the dreamer. C. G. Jung referred to this as the "aha" response. It indicates that consciousness has seen and been nourished by the wisdom of the dream. But this is usually only an introduction to the real work with the dream—only a gate to the task of integrating the image into our souls, essential for the soul's unfolding. After recognizing, for example, that the wounded cat in a dream reflects an aspect of our own wounded feline instincts, it is necessary to move toward the cat with such empathy that we become the cat, assuming her limbs and posture, living so completely in her skin that we can see the world through her eyes and feel it through her wounds. Then, and only then, can healing and transformation occur.

Sometimes the dream, by indicating the nature of the wounds, acts as an invitation to this process of compassionate acceptance and integration. At other times, as in the following dream which accompanied and reflected Sally's increasing compassion for her own wounded instincts, the dream images signify the completion of a process.

Sally dreamed that she was walking through her childhood village with her brother when she came to three wounded and bound cats lying on the other side of the road. She crossed over to help them. Since it was quickly apparent that they were dying of thirst, she

*walked to a nearby well and drew several buckets of water, which
she carefully carried to the thirsty cats. Then she untied the ropes
which were binding them. As the cats were freed they turned into
three large and powerful black men who thanked her for her consideration. Delighted by their transformation, she invited the men to
come home with her for a meal.*

The act of feeling and receiving the quality and essence of the
dream image is necessary, whatever its nature. A fascist torturer may
be as much a part of our unconscious as a Chinese sage. And if his
cruelty and ruthlessness are to have a possibility of transformation,
they need to be sufficiently recognized and absorbed to enable us
to experience his evil from both sides, as subject and object: to suffer
his carefully executed torments, as well as listen for his motivations
in executing them. It is necessary to feel the pain as well as the
shame of harboring him within our soul.

Natural images in dreams also invite our communion with them.
The old oak tree on the front lawn may appear as something other,
something outside of us when seen with physical eyes, or from the
perspective of the dreamer, whose consciousness usually reflects his
waking view of himself and the world. But as we begin imaginatively
to merge with the tree—to enter its branches, to stretch ourselves
along its limbs, to move down its trunk into the earth, feeling the
sap traveling through the roots deep into the dark, moist soil and
rising up toward the sun—the tree spontaneously reveals itself as an
essential and inalienable part of us.

Working with dreams and waking images in this way is a form of
meditation. It requires a disciplined and receptive contemplation of
the image until we reach a place in which all consciousness of things
other than it is lost, and we are at one with the image itself. Through
such deep imaginative communion we are healed and transformed.

Chapter Three

MARRIAGE OF HEAVEN AND EARTH

As the language of the soul, reflecting and relating both poles of our existence, heaven and earth, spirit and form, images bridge these opposites, allowing experience of each. And like soul, the imagination is creative not only in its own realm, but also through its impact on the worlds it mirrors and connects: an erotic image arouses the body; an image of God awakens the spirit. Without this bridge of soul and the imagination, consciousness is imprisoned within one or other of the two poles of being, within the intellect and physical world or within the formless realm of spirit. By way of soul and the imagination, spirit and form can communicate with and be touched by each other. We can expand our reach, know and feel our wholeness.

For as long as wounds and desires remain unacknowledged and unfelt, the images of heaven and earth, spirit and earth which live at their core remain inaccessible to consciousness. But as pains and hungers begin to be admitted into consciousness, they bring with them the universal images which underlie the personal and particular: as the cruel mother image is recognized and suffered, her cruelty dissolves, unveiling an original benevolence; the hypercritical domineering bigot dissolves unveiling the gentle, wise guide; "God" loses his authoritarian glance; the cat is healed of her sickness; and the withered tree sprouts fresh leaves. As a physical wound, once cleansed and exposed to air, begins to heal, so psychological wounds, brought into the air of consciousness and cleansed by our tears and shame, spontaneously heal themselves, enabling a whole limb to emerge in place of the disfigured one, a benevolent being in place of the demonic one. For evil, in all its forms, is created and perpetuated by our flight from suffering. In order to escape from the unacknowledged pain of a childhood rejection, for example, we dismiss, condemn, or attack anyone or anything which threatens to remind us of this wound. In turning toward our pain we deprive these ugly mechanisms and sub-personalities of the energy they need to survive. This process of soul-finding and healing is long and laborious. It requires patient attentiveness and respect for each waking or dreamed image, each emotion, and all discordant thoughts as a potential opportunity to participate in our becoming.

In the imaginative world, the physical distinctions of inner and outer, I and it, cease to be meaningful. For as the images are integrated into consciousness, tree, bird, child, or mountain cease to feel outside or other and become inherent aspects of our being. We might choose to observe the physical tree as something other or touch it with our physical senses to prove its otherness. But the moment we begin to explore its essence, its treeness, the barriers of otherness dissolve, and we find ourselves in the presence of Tree. Not the tree on a lawn or even a tree inside a soul, but the Tree which can manifest as both a physical tree and as the Tree of Life which invigorates soul, the archetypal Tree.

In this way the dismembered parts of our being are re-membered. And each re-membering increases and heals our capacity for relationship. Dissociated from consciousness by painful childhood experiences or memories from other times—the negative mother wound, for example—alienates us from mother, both individual mother and Mother Nature, body and earth, and thereby obstructs our capacity to receive the sap of life as it ascends from the earth through body and into soul. It inhibits our capacity for maternal feelings and actions, for unconditional acceptance of another, for receiving, allowing, and nourishing. In flight from this wound we are likely not only to resist mothering our children, unconsciously resentful of the mothering we never received, but also to reject our bodies, refusing to inhabit them and take our physical place as integral parts of Mother Earth.

If anyone had asked Sally about her relationship to her body before she had become involved in her inner journey, she would probably have replied that she liked her body and was glad to inhabit it. Not knowing anything else, she imagined that all the attention she gave to her body, all the grooming and careful dressing, meant she liked and enjoyed living in it. What she did not realize then was that taking care of a body, attending to its health through exercise and wise nutrition, and clothing it attractively do not necessarily indicate a conscious acceptance and enjoyment of its physicality. The nature of the difference revealed itself to her one winter evening as she relaxed in a steaming bath.

Sally often took long baths on cold evenings, using them as a time to reflect on the day's events, on her dreams. . . . But this evening she found herself simply looking at her body. She noticed its beauty—the slender waist, elegant limbs; but also its ugliness—thighs becoming dimpled with age, breasts beginning to droop. She noticed the few stray hairs growing where she would have preferred they did not, the birthmarks, the awkward moles on her shoulder. But instead of wondering, as she had done so often before, how she could improve this body, make it more beautiful in her eyes and the eyes of others, Sally felt a quiet tenderness toward it, an acceptance and compassion for its unique combination of perfection and imperfection. She noticed and enjoyed its femininity as she stretched down into its legs, arms, and fingers. And, for the first time, she was able to acknowledge them as the embodiment of her, to feel them as her earthly home.

Slowly she began to wash, and though the pattern of her movements was probably similar to that of countless previous baths, it felt different now. For she was not washing out of duty, nor out of a desire to smell fresh, but because she wanted to take care of her body, to give it the cleanliness it needed, to listen to and attend to its well-being. She washed it gently, tenderly stroking its aging skin.

When she stepped out of the bath that evening, she felt that she was standing on the earth for the first time.

As the negative mother wound is met and suffered by way of attending to those events, images, and people who prick it into life, a new capacity to live in our body, to enjoy its beauty and to lovingly accept its imperfections arises within us. Fat legs or crooked noses that we spent decades wishing into oblivion return to us as essential parts of who we are, asking for and receiving our acceptance and compassion. We begin to listen to what our body wants rather than imposing ideals or goals upon it; to attend to its well-being through rest and exercise, to provide it with the food it needs, and clothe it in shapes and colors in tune with its nature.

We also become able to listen to it, feeling for areas where the flow of energy is obstructed or excessive, and assisting in the restoration of its health. Often these pockets of tension, low vitality, or overheating reflect unconscious psychological wounds, which—once invited into consciousness and allowed to heal, spontaneously restore the body to health. But sometimes, even after the psychological work has occurred, the physical reflection of the wound remains intact, locked into place by years of tension and dis-ease. In these cases direct healing work with the body, always useful as a companion to psychological healing, becomes essential. Massage, relaxation techniques, and homeopathic medications need to be used in conjunction with healing visualizations to provide the dis-eased part of the body with thoughts and images of health. If it is necessary also to make use of allopathic medicine—drugs and surgery—it is helpful not to hand over our bodies to the doctor and the treatments, but rather by remembering that our bodies are not objects, things outside of us to be fixed by others, to honor them as living images of our souls, requiring compassion, understanding, and cooperation if they are to find health. (It is also useful to choose doctors who share this perspective on healing, a gynecologist, for example, who relates to our bodies neither as clinical specimens nor as erotic objects but as the garment of our souls.)

The capacity to distinguish between body reality and soul reality is one of the gifts born from listening to and suffering through psychological wounds and desires. For as psychic hunger becomes distinct from physical hunger, psychic desires distinct from physical ones, the body is relieved of the burden of being used to satisfy emotional desires or anesthetize fears. The compulsive eater, for example, no longer needs to stuff her body in the attempt to find psychological nourishment; the compulsive jogger can go easy on his body as he discovers that psychological worth and meaning are not identical to physical youth and prowess. And as the body becomes differentiated from the soul, the task of caring for it becomes less onerous. For, once released from psychological projections, the body's demands are quite simple. It needs sleep, healthy food, exercise; it needs to be washed and cared for. But no more. It has no unacceptable demands. We do not need to control it, to deny it or educate it into obedience—only to care for it and to go about our soul business. Then, instead of being experienced through the lenses of our wounds, the body begins to exist in its own right. It becomes both more and less important: less important as a means of satisfying psychological needs, and more important for what it is—something of beauty and value, the earthly expression of our soul.

Once we have accepted our body as it is and have allowed ourselves to reach down into it, owning and inhabiting it, rather than just using it, it becomes possible to know and relate to the earth as our greater body: possible to descend into its vast depths and spaces; to enter its rivers, merging with their waters as they slide over boulders and through narrow gulleys; to imaginatively drink the sap rising in the trees; to enter the petals of the daffodil and be filled by their yellowness; and to sink into the molten core of earth, into the rocks and mountains, absorbing their strength and power.

Once we can begin to recognize and experience the earth as the inseparable extension of and womb of our bodies, we are unlikely to choose to mistreat, abuse, or pollute her. Feeding her soil toxic chemicals begins to feel as inappropriate as feeding our body toxic foods. Polluting it with refuse seems as unattractive as walking about unwashed, in rags. The earth, experienced as our earth, the mother and web of our body, becomes a source of energy we can consciously call on when our individual body is depleted. We can drink in the peaceful energy of nature just as the body drinks a glass of water, receiving it through the pores of our being. But the reverse is also true. Destructive, discordant environments, as well as those sustained by a lower frequency of being, a darker presence than our own individual energy field, can sap our energy unless we consciously turn off our receptive faculties which at other moments enable us to merge into and be enlivened by the fields and forests. And when even this turning off is not enough, it can be helpful to invite inspiring and life-filled images of light and love to surround and wash through us, asking them to dissolve the destructive energy.

Since, like all opposites, heaven and earth, spirit and body spontaneously attract each other in their unending search for wholeness and equilibrium, an experience of body invites an experience of spirit. But before the wealth of the spirit can be creatively integrated into our earthly life, it is necessary to meet and suffer those wounds associated with the father and other patriarchal or spiritual figures. Unsuffered, these wounds obstruct our capacity to allow the eternal and transcendent to permeate individual feeling and relating. A negative father wound, for example, will inhibit, contaminate, and distort our capacity to perceive and receive the eternal Father. For our souls are the mirrors and vessels whereby we communicate with and reflect our archetypal nature. Inasmuch as they are distorted by ugly and wounded figures, our reflections of truth and being will be correspondingly distorted.

If this essential psychological work does not take place, it is, of course, possible to have spiritual experiences, even profound and illuminating ones. But such experiences are likely to remain isolated from the rest of our being, unintegrated into our individuality and therefore unable to be reflected in our relationships with others and with the earth. Moreover, without sufficient psychological discrimination to disentangle our wounds and wounded perceptions from reality, it is tempting to gather spiritual truths into the service of our individual flight from pain: to judge and condemn another's actions rather than own and suffer the pain these actions awake in us. As Sally's marriage to Luke deteriorated, he provided her with a painful and illuminating example of the spiritualization of psychological pain.

During their years together their mutual interest in spiritual realities, which had once enlivened their relationship, began to suffocate it. For when either felt the relationship to be inadequate and unfulfilling in some area, they had become accustomed to avoiding the dissatisfaction by focusing on their spiritual interests. Recently Sally had found it hard to quiet her psychological hungers in this old way, but at the same time difficult not to identify with Luke's condemnation of these hungers as not only selfish but a betrayal of the sacred bond of marriage. Somewhere she dimly sensed something questionable in his implicit assumption that serving the spirit was synonymous with serving their marriage, but so loud was his judging voice that she rarely dared to give more than a fleeting moment to this question.

Occasionally she risked talking to him about the dry, unfeeling nature of their relating, the routine days of habits and duties. But usually he would respond by berating her for her lack of discipline and reverence toward their marriage vows. Occasionally he acknowledged the fear and pain which their deteriorating relationship provoked in him, but mostly he adopted the position toward her of spiritual instructor, criticizing and judging her from a position of superiority. She tended to leave these discussions doubting the validity of her hungers and feeling somewhat guilty for not being able to live up to her spiritual ideals.

One evening as she saw him walk through the door, depleted by a long day of composing, she felt a cramp of fear and horror in her stomach at the cruel cunning she saw on his face. Horror that this ugly person was someone she had once loved and married. As he hugged her, she responded out of habit, but inwardly she recoiled. They went upstairs to the sitting room, where she managed to sit as far away from him as possible. Fortunately, that evening he had a lot to talk to her about. Much had happened in his day, new musical ideas had arisen and a new student had come to him, drawn by the evident spirituality underlying his music.

Not listening to his words, Sally took the time to look more closely at the cruel figure sitting opposite her. And the more she looked the greater her terror. In the midst of her pain she noticed, to her astonishment, that this ghastly being had begun to acquire a life of its own, was becoming something separate from the man sitting on the chair. The apparition grew until she found herself in the presence of two people—her husband and a demonic being. Still unable to concentrate on what was being said to her, she continued to watch and experience this image of cruelty, to feel its force and cunning malice. The pain became so great that for a while she doubted that she had the strength to withstand it. But as she watched, raw and shaken, she noticed the image beginning to dissolve, becoming limp and small, dissipating into air. Only then did she realize with shame as well as relief that she had just encountered an aspect of herself, nourished by her fear of meeting her wounds and feeling her hungers, and locked in place by her fear of seeing it. She looked across the room. Her husband, whom she loved but no longer wished to live with, was still sitting in his chair, still talking, his face no longer masked by the reflection of her own judgmental demon.

Once this negative projection had been withdrawn it became increasingly easy for Sally to listen to her own needs and to acknowledge the dry, unfeeling nature of the marriage. She tried to talk to Luke about it, but each time she was met with more condemnation and criticism, more oughts and shoulds and moral imperatives. Finally she decided to respect her needs and leave their arid relationship. "I feel sorry for you," he said when she told him of her decision. "You will certainly have to meet our relationship in another lifetime so that you may resolve the problems you are now choosing to escape."

Often, during the long months which preceded their divorce, she heard his words reverberating within her. Often she was tempted to believe them, to replace the loneliness and pain created by honoring her own needs and perceptions in the presence of his condemnation and criticism with a new commitment to their marriage, tempted to avoid the suffering of standing beside her decision with her feelings, regardless of how her husband and his friends chose to see and judge her.

As a defense against acknowledging his own pain, Luke maintained his spiritually superior position to the final day of their marriage, rarely allowing himself to touch his own wounds. On the morning of their divorce, he greeted her in the courtroom with the words "I feel so sorry for you to see you here."

As important as suffering the wounds associated with painful father and patriarchal figures is acknowledging and absorbing positive spiritual projections—remembering moments when we were so inspired by a spiritual teacher, a priest, or a monk that, momentarily or perhaps longer, we fell in love with him, and entering again that ecstasy, feeling our soul ennobled, enlightened, and nourished by the experience. Such work helps to separate the spiritual image from those who appear to carry and reflect it. It prepares the soil of soul to receive the seeds of spirit.

Whereas it is relatively simple to move into body and earth once the psychological images of mother and matter have been retrieved, cleansed, and healed by imaginative work, and to gain access to the soul through attention to the feeling qualities of images, it is not so simple to move into spirit. For unlike the physical and psychological bodies, the spiritual body, the transcendent source of light and truth, is neither immediately visible nor palpable. Long and patient exercises are often necessary to unfold and refine our spiritual organs of perception. This is the work of meditation, prayer, and contemplation. Different spiritual traditions advocate different forms of meditation—mantras, chanting, sacred dance, contemplation of spiritual images, pondering spiritual texts and many others. Which form we choose depends essentially on personal inclination and the stage of our spiritual unfolding. Each, in its way, can feed our spiritual hunger and refine our perception. And, as this happens, exercises which initially felt dry and arduous begin to feel vital and unmistakably satisfying. We begin to look forward to meditation as much as, if not more than, we might look forward to a delicious meal.

After a time, a new longing arises within the soul, a longing for the spirit uncluttered by meditative techniques; a longing which seems to invite a complete emptying of soul, a dying of all striving and exertion until nothing is left but a quiet and tender receptivity. As the trying to concentrate, the trying to listen or achieve diminishes, as the tension which creates and defines our separateness fades, a conscious merging with the spirit becomes possible so that, for brief, quiet moments, its radiance becomes our radiance, and its peace our peace.

As consciousness reconnects with the psychological images of heaven and earth, suffering their distortions and wounds sufficiently to enable healing and transformation, the psychological bridge between the two poles of our being awakens into consciousness. Its center is the heart. Positioned midway between spirit and earth, head and feet, the heart can relate and receive the energies of each— the vitality of the body and the enlightening radiance of the spirit. As the center of soul, the heart presides over our marriage of heaven and earth, transforming the polarization of body and spirit into creative relationship.

Without the connecting center of the heart we tend to move somewhat dramatically between spirit and earth. In women this condition often manifests as an oscillation between nun and whore. For deprived of access to the integrating heart center, such women reach for their fulfillment by way of their two poles, body and spirit, involvement with one spontaneously inviting involvement with the other. They may have eroticism and spirituality, but little love or conscious relating.

But as we listen to our emotions and feelings, accept and admit them into consciousness, the wounded, dismembered, and scarred parts of our selves gradually heal, and our heart, no longer aching and rigid, becomes able to transmit love. The process can be seen as the emergence of the individual cross: the axis between body and spirit, physiologically reflected by the spine, crossed by the axis of relationship expressed by the arms. By way of the vertical we are able to connect to heaven and earth, and by way of the horizontal to individuals and humanity. The source of both axes exists as the dimensionless point where they touch.

As Sally's heart center was opening and healing, and as her capacity to relate to the reality of another—rather than merely in response to her own wounded, hungry, and unconscious needs— was therefore becoming more accessible to her, she dreamed that *the risen Christ and Saint Peter confined to a giant seesaw in the*

*courtyard of a castle and tormented by being made to seesaw inces-
santly. The Virgin Mary appeared and, moved with compassion for
their suffering, dug into the hillside with her bare hands to divert a
stream. As the waters rushed through the castle walls toward the
seesaw, they brought new life to Christ and Peter, releasing them
from their torment. The seesaw stilled itself, and Christ was able to
walk in freedom through the leaf-strewn courtyard.*

Until the marriage between heaven and earth, thinking and doing,
body and spirit becomes a reality, until the center of the individual
soul, which alone can mediate between the opposites, is found and
claimed, the two poles of our being remain confined by their lack
of relationship with each other, tormented by the unending swing of
the pendulum, forever deprived of peace and equilibrium. The Virgin
Mary symbolizes the vessel of soul which is sufficiently cleansed of
personal desires and unconscious wounds to be able to experience
and relate to both body and spirit, to the rock of earth, Saint Peter,
and to the risen Christ, our divine nature. Her compassion enables
her to undertake the arduous task of diverting the life-bringing waters
into the courtyard, to enable the flow of life to enter the castle of
our soul and replace arid and painful polarization with the vital and
creative possibilities of relationship between spirit and body, heaven
and earth.

Chapter Four

BIRTH OF SELF

On that cold March day when Sally dialed the number of a Jungian therapist she was actively acknowledging the existence of a dark, mysterious world underlying her consciousness, a world as significant a part of her being as (or perhaps more significant than) her conscious collection of thoughts, feelings, and passionate convictions. She was recognizing the need to listen to her own oppressed parts, before she could know how to help the world's oppressed people; to find her own freedom, before she could assist the freedom of others.

The nature of individual consciousness is composed of a unique mixture of personal, historical, cultural, geographical, and biological influences. It is the lens through which we view the world and our relationships to others. A lens which can only see what it is focused to see.

There is a story, possibly apocryphal, that when the Spaniards first arrived with their horses in the New World the natives thought that they were mythical beings, half human and half animal, since they had no conceptual or imaginative framework in their consciousness to enable them to perceive horses. In some ways we are no less blind than those Native Americans, for we are unable to experience what our conscious thoughts, opinions, prejudices, and passions do not permit us to experience.

Although the conscious mind does not remain static but changes constantly from birth to death, continually altered by the inclusion of new experiences, insights, and information, we nevertheless tend to identify with this fluctuating world, reluctant to acknowledge its relative position and status, its dependence on a vast reservoir of unconscious reality and authority.

The following Sufi tale illustrates the illusory power and status of those who have forgotten the foundation and source of their being:

> The man had lived alone in the house for many years. It was a big house, containing many luxurious rooms, and he enjoyed using these to entertain his friends. He slept in the master bedroom and delighted in all the comforts and amenities the house offered him. When decisions needed to be made about the house, when it needed repairs or renovations, he would go into the coffers stored in the basement and take all the gold necessary to pay for the work. And so his life continued, seemingly untroubled. But one evening, as he was sitting in front of the large fireplace, relaxing after an excellent dinner, a noble and dignified man descended the main staircase. Suddenly the one beside the fire remembered . . . . He remembered that the newcomer was the true master of the house and he only a servant, placed in charge during his master's absence.

It is an uncomfortable moment for the individual ego-consciousness, that part of us identified with the ephemeral world of body and personality, to discover that it is not the master of soul but merely a faithful or, more often, unfaithful servant. As the truth begins to surface, the conscious personality is tempted to make use of time-honored methods of denial, repression, and dissociation in the attempt to maintain rather than relinquish its illusory control. And our society offers many tools and weapons to assist it in its battle—many positive-thinking exercises, meditation techniques, mutual support groups and counseling approaches designed to buttress the ego's power, to fortify it against the unconscious and the still voice of its master, the Self.

If this battle continues for too long, it may produce physical symptoms, for energies denied access to consciousness have a tendency to become locked in the body, manifesting themselves as physical ailments and disease. Such a battle also depletes the conscious personality by depriving it of the necessary food for its own renewal, for psychological well-being depends on the continual influx of new ideas, feelings, and vitality from the unconscious. Inasmuch as the ego personality seeks, consciously or otherwise, to maintain control, to hold fast to the status quo, it locks the gates to its own growth and revitalization. It dams the rejuvenating flow from spirit and earth into body and soul.

Our egos are like islands surrounded by the eternal and infinite ocean. For a while, perhaps even for decades, these islands have sufficient food to sustain us. But at a certain moment, different for each person, the island's resources are exhausted. Then we have only two possibilities. We can choose to remain within the limits of the island, eking out a marginal existence amid such familiar signs of psychological starvation as boredom, cynicism, resignation, and contempt, or we can venture into the ocean; risk the hidden terrors of the deep in search of new land and new life.

After years of creating and fortifying our island habitation, it is frightening to acknowledge its limits, to recognize its dependence on the unknown ocean. Leaving the familiar island shores to enter this unfamiliar sea requires the capacity to respect our hunger and thirst; the courage to relinquish attempts to control our environment and destiny; and the humility to meet and accept the unconscious universe of soul, acknowledging its will as the will of Self. The loss of pride is considerable. From being the one who controlled, initiated, organized, and ordered, ego becomes the listener, the follower, the humble servant, whose tasks are cooperation and obedience, not dictatorship and oppression.

The unconscious includes not only everything we have denied or rejected as either too painful or incompatible with our conscious image of ourselves, of nature and spirit, but also the unknown and unremembered, the seeds of our becoming. These depend on consciousness for the nourishment essential to their unfolding. Without the interest, the questions and listening of the conscious mind, these seeds cannot germinate and grow. For questions and answers not only constellate but depend on each other. Going to sleep with a question is likely to produce a helpful dream from the unconscious. Meditating with a question is likely to bring guidance. When we do not ask the question there is no vacuum to receive the reply. When we do, answers as well as new branches of our being emerge in their appropriate manner and time. Often we have to grow, to expand and strengthen our capacity for hearing and feeling by holding the tension of our conflicts and unknowing before we can hear and feel their resolution and elucidation.

This sometimes joyous and sometimes painful relationship between conscious and unconscious creates a path between our spirits and bodies whereby we can know and experience our wholeness. The emergence of this channel to our greater being invites us to replace my will with Thy Will, the will of the body-bound personality with the will of our eternal being; and to recognize that Thy Will is not something other and outer but the essential core of our being, the call of our soul hungry for the realization of its own divinity. At many moments in our lives, even in childhood, we are prepared for this recognition and surrender to the way of soul.

Sally's early years were rhythmically punctuated with religious moments. There was church on Sundays, prayers kneeling at her mother's knees before bed, and grace before and after each meal. But none of these events consciously awoke her to the divine grandeur of the human soul. Her awakening occurred one weekday morning as she sat alone in the chapel of her convent school. The mass was finished, and only the lingering smell of incense remained to testify to the early morning bustle of nuns and young communicants filing their way to the altar. Sally had watched them from her knees, unable to receive the paper white host since she had been baptized in the Church of England. But now they were gone, and she was alone in the chapel. She did not ask herself why she had chosen to come back instead of playing with her friends. Her ten-year-old mind was not troubled by such questions. It was enough to be there, to drink in the stillness, and to enjoy the freedom of her choice. For no one had told her to come. Indeed, the nuns would have been surprised to see a Protestant voluntarily entering the chapel. They might have secretly smiled at the thought of a possible conversion. But she was not interested in being converted. Indeed, it did not matter to her which religious label she possessed. What did matter was that she could come to the chapel, alone, undisturbed by the chatter of friends and the supervision of teachers.

She walked to one of the side pews and knelt down, fervently hoping that no one would intrude upon her aloneness. She looked at the gilt statues of Christ and the Virgin Mary on the altar. Then she left her pew and walked slowly around the fourteen stations of the cross, as she had seen her Catholic friends do, looking at each for a moment, and then moving on, until she came to the final scenes of the crucifixion. Here she paused, stirred by the enormity of Christ's sacrifice.

Returning to her pew, she knelt down. The chapel's silence seemed louder now. It pierced the top of her head and flowed into her heart, feeding her with an unknown and familiar joy.

Having drunk in all the silence she could contain, she left the chapel, taking with her a new satisfaction and a new hunger. Stepping outside into the warm summer air, she saw some of her friends moving toward the tennis courts. In her eagerness to join them, she forgot the still moments in the chapel. And did not remember them for many years.

Such moments unconsciously prepare our souls for the later, more conscious journey of unfolding and the essential surrender of my will to Thine, ego will to the will of Self, by providing a sense of something infinitely greater, more powerful and more joyous than that available to the ego-personality alone.

The collapse of the ego's sense of superiority and control provides a foretaste of physical death. For after the intense suffering of our wounds, the recognition and integration of aspects of our psychological masculinity and femininity, and the sadness which inevitably accompanies the withdrawal of projections, there follows a much deeper depression: days, perhaps months, in which we feel everything has been drained from us—our capacity to choose, our sense of security and value—everything which has kept us afloat as seemingly autonomous individuals. Sometimes the only intruder into this darkness is doubt, quick to mock and question the purpose of the journey; quick to tempt us to return to the old ways of ego control, when depression and humility could be ignored or deflected.

Sally was lying on her bed, the curtains drawn against the light.

"Maybe there is nothing in the darkness, just more and more darkness, until life ebbs away in futility," she thought. "How do I know that I am on the right path? I have been trusting my therapist. How do I know that she knows and understands what's happening to me? Perhaps she has just read about it in books without ever experiencing it for herself. Perhaps Jung never even experienced it either, just guessed at it all. What about my friends who think I am becoming a little crazy? Perhaps they are right. Perhaps it would be better to rejoin the social cycle of parties and movies. Perhaps it is a little foolish to spend day after day watching the walls of my psychological house crumbling into ruin."

On and on, Doubt spoke to Sally, relentless in its attempt to get her to turn back. Sometimes she found herself answering "yes" to these doubting questions, tired of the sadness and loneliness, the darkness which blanketed her days. But when she tried to turn around, her old life felt empty, devoid of vitality and interest. So she returned to the darkness.

Her analyst could not do very much to support her during these days, except to be there, a continually loving presence, exuding a certain confidence that the end of the darkness would not be more darkness. The little analytic consulting room with its two large leather chairs became a haven for her from the loneliness of her house and the well-intended but useless advice of those friends visibly frightened by her descent into depression.

In the midst of the darkness, she dreamed she was visited by an ageless blind man. Somewhat alarmed by his demeanor, she tried to bolt the door. But doors did not seem to pose an obstacle to this strange figure. He just walked through them. Accepting the inevitability of his entrance, she moved toward him, and they touched each other with warmth.

In their touching, the blindness of the ageless, unconscious wisdom connected with the limited light of consciousness. And both were transformed. Sally's fear of letting in new wisdom from the unconscious had been the fear of the radical changes this would bring—changes beside which even the long days of depression might seem preferable. She had feared who and what she might discover in the darkness, feared her own becoming, the responsibility for it and the demands it might make on her. Part of her wanted to cling to the old wounds, the neuroses and insecurities which had characterized her previous existence, for at least they were familiar, relatively safe compared to the unknown possibilities of a new and larger life.

But after meeting the ageless old man, the darkness changed and her fears diminished. She felt the old man's arms around her, holding her as she fell deeper into the unknown. She felt herself embraced and protected by his presence. She began to relax, to allow some of the tension and exhaustion of the years of trying to be independent and autonomous to dissolve. And remembering that "the wisdom of this world is foolishness in the eyes of God," she recognized the doubting voice as the voice of "this world," the voice of the status quo, enlivened by her fear of pain and transformation.

The following night she dreamed she was in labor. The midwife told her to lie on her back, not on her stomach. And the next night she dreamed she was in Japan with Patrick, her brother-in-law. They were clearing the last remnants of rubbish and placing them in garbage cans. All around they felt the world hovering on the edge of nuclear disaster. Passers-by speculated on their chances of survival even while sensing there would be no survivors. Sally and Patrick went into a bomb shelter, an old ruin filled with people crouching in corners and behind boulders, seeking an impossible protection. Looking around, Sally saw a door. She opened it, expecting to see the mushroom cloud of the atomic bomb and the imminent destruction of the world. Instead she saw Mount Fujiyama rising from the ocean, its summit a shimmering pink in the pale dawn light, circled by five spiraling rainbows. As she enjoyed its beauty, she heard God's words to Noah that never again would he send a flood to destroy the earth, and that the rainbow was to be a token of His promise.

A few nights later she dreamed she descended from the summit of a mountain to the bed of a lake, where she saw God sitting on a golden throne.

Her descent into her own dark depths had sufficiently dissolved the illusory shadows of ego identity for her to realize the divine as living not only as the infinite realm of spirit but also as the source and substance of her own body and soul. Thy Will was no longer something outside, something to be found in temples and churches, to be heard through the words of sacred texts. Its presence and voice had become directly accessible to her from within.

The sacrifice of control by the ego consciousness often feels like a cataclysm, like the end of the world. For from the perspective of ego this is exactly what it is—a collapse of the old ways of strife, manipulation, domination, and single-minded pursuit of egoistic ideals. What the ego cannot see before the destruction of its despotic regime is the beauty of the new order which emerges from the ruins of the old—the inspiring grandeur of the mountain of Self which arises into consciousness once our little body-bound wills have relinquished their attempts at despotic control.

Sally's work with her dreams had laid the psychological foundations for the birth into consciousness of her divine Self. This occurred
one morning in meditation.

For about four weeks Sally had felt a tension mounting within her
as though something enormous were pressing against the parameters
of her consciousness asking to be admitted. Although she had no
idea what the thing was, its touch excited and inspired her, and she
found herself spontaneously remembering a postcard of Holman
Hunt's painting of Christ knocking at the door which she had been
given by the school vicar on the eve of her confirmation. Though
she had never much liked the painting she had always kept it, moved
by the image it evoked in her as well as by the biblical quotation
the vicar had written beneath it: "Behold, I stand at the door and
knock. If any man hear my voice, and open the door, I will come
into him, and will sup with him, and he with me." (Revelations
3:20).

Now it was Easter week and at least twenty years since she had
received the card. Sally was visiting the Spanish towns of Avila and
Toledo, walking the streets once walked by Saint Theresa and her
friend, Saint John of the Cross. The local people were busy preparing
their Easter celebrations, parading large and often crudely sculptured
statues of Christ in candlelit procession through the cobbled streets.
As she joined a congregation for the Good Friday service, she had
no difficulty immersing herself in the experience of darkness as the
candles were ritually extinguished to symbolize Christ's death.

On Easter Saturday she moved away from the crowds to the house
of a friend on the edge of the Mediterranean, in order to celebrate
alone.

Easter Sunday arrived in a still crisp light. For a while Sally lay in
bed, enjoying the quiet emptiness of the house and the warmth of
the generous layers of blankets. Then she felt the familiar tension
again pressing in on her with a new urgency and power. She sat up
cross-legged in her flannel nightgown to give the experience her
complete attention. And then it happened. She felt herself instanta-
neously absorbed and permeated by an ecstatic, eternal, and universal love. The image which came to her was no longer Christ
knocking on the closed door but of Christ having entered, having
come home after long years of knocking.

Initially the ecstasy was so great that tears of release dampened
the collar of her nightgown. She sat in shock—a new person seeing

and feeling a new world. The bed and walls, even the patch of ocean through the window, seemed as much a part of her now as the unhurried beating of her heart. In that moment she felt she had everything she had ever wanted. There no longer seemed to be anything outside of herself. She had become inseparable from everything and every person. She was everything and everyone just as they were her. And along with this knowing she also knew that this everything that she was had an individual existence as Sally and an individual life to live, one which would henceforth be committed to serving the everything that it was.

The experience remained with her in its original intensity for three days and then it began to fade, overlaid by Sally-oriented attitudes, thoughts, and feelings. But it never entirely vanished; it remained more or less accessible to her when she remembered to turn toward it, a constant reminder that her being was simultaneously unique and universal.

After she returned from Spain and was preparing to visit her analyst again, she began to look for words with which to express her experience. In the midst of her ponderings she remembered a man she had known when she was seventeen who had periods of thinking he was God. The memory confused her. For she realized that the same words "I am God" could be used by both of them.

It was her analyst who helped to sort out her confusion by describing her friend's mania as ego inflation, a state of being during which the body- and personality-bound ego consciousness identifies itself with God or Self, equating its own separateness with divinity. She explained that this was quite different from Sally's experience, in which her consciousness had so fully relinquished its identity with Sally's body and ephemeral personality that it was able to return and unite with its source and could do so without losing its vital and creative relationship to the individual cell of this cosmic being known as Sally.

The realization of our wholeness and divinity, the birth of Self, is the first major initiation of the soul. The term "initiation" is increasingly being used by psychotherapists and others in association with significant moments of psychological transformation, whether these are constellated by outer events, (like marriage, divorce, death, or even an examination), or brought about largely by inner processes. While this more general use of the term would appear to be justified in view of the word's derivation from the Latin *in* ("into") and *ire* ("to go"), its popularization nevertheless deprives us of a concept with which to describe the much rarer crises of soul-becoming. Those events, perhaps lasting no more than a few minutes, decisively conclude one period of becoming, terminate one level of consciousness, and begin, initiate, another and greater one.

The distinction between psychological transformation and initiation may be clarified a little by the metaphor of moving house. The soul's journey toward increased consciousness can be regarded as a process of moving from one psychological home to another. Much time and energy is spent finding and gathering the raw materials, locating the appropriate land, recognizing the design of the house, laying the foundations, constructing and transforming it. This is the long, slow work of psychological integration, change, and transformation which characterizes the greater part of our unfolding. But occasionally, very rarely, maybe not more than once in a lifetime, the time arrives to leave our old house and move into the new one we have worked so hard to prepare. Such radical and fundamental moves have their beginnings in initiations.

Through dreams, visions, active imagination, and meditation we may perceive the possibility, even the location and design, of a new home; intuit its topography; perhaps travel to its land; glimpse the view from its window; and experience a re-membering, a recognition of a long-forgotten place. But, while these forays, these temporary journeys abroad, may prepare us for the eventual move, they are psychologically distinct from the move itself.

Every initiation involves a complete reorientation of consciousness, a redefinition of and a new relationship to Self. As we prepare to move into the larger home, the old one which housed us for so many years begins to collapse. And, with an unshakable knowledge, we know it would be impossible to reconstruct and reinhabit it without feeling diminished and cramped, in every way less than who we have become by way of the initiation.

Long before the birth of Self we can sense its approach as an invitation and a longing to move deeper into the stillness of our being; to move into and through the painful, raw, and jagged parts of ourselves so that they may find their healing, and, in so doing, unveil the wholeness of Self. This is the way characterized by the I–Thou relationship, during which the ego consciousness listens to and serves the greater will of soul becoming. With the birth of Self we experience for the first time our I uniting with the Thou. We recognize ourselves as, in essence, the star, not merely the one who serves and follows it.

Like a physical birth, the birth of Self brings us new responsibilities, new difficulties, as well as new gifts and possibilities. Our infant being requires much sensitive listening and attention if its needs are to be met, its nature watered and nourished. Moreover, these needs, once discerned, often appear to conflict, even contradict, the interests and needs of the outer world—of one's family, friends, and society. To ignore or neglect the infant Self in the interest of avoiding pain, conflict, and recrimination is to find ourselves washed up on the river banks of our own becoming: arid, bored, and stifled by meaninglessness and exhaustion.

To remain loyal to the unfolding Self is to risk rejection and loneliness. For even those closest to us cannot hear directly the voice of our own Self. We are alone with our dreams, meditations, and feelings. Someone conversant with the language of soul may be able to support us at this time by recognizing and affirming the validity of our perceptions, but the ultimate responsibility and sense of truth is ours alone. It is not comfortable to stand unsupported, cradling one's infant Self in a world which cannot see or hear it and therefore has little respect or understanding for its needs. But the pain and loneliness test and strengthen our capacity to listen to the voice of soul, rather than the voices of convention and collective morality.

About a year after the Spanish experience which brought her Self to consciousness, Sally began to receive dreams indicating that she needed to leave her home and move to the United States. Initially, of course, she explored the possible symbolic meanings of these dreams to discover whether the move needed to be a physical or a psychological one, or both. She pondered her associations with America, attempting to acquire a sense of it as a country of her soul. But this exclusively symbolic approach failed to elicit the "aha" response. It failed to provide her with a sense that she had understood and grown by way of the dreams. And, as if to confirm that she had not yet understood them, the dreams continued to arrive. So she decided to explore the possibility that the move needed to happen on the earth as well as in her soul.

At first this idea was quite appealing. She had been attracted to the United States for many years, and she enjoyed traveling. But before long the less attractive implications of such a move also surfaced into consciousness. It would mean taking Rachael, now ten, away from her school and, more importantly, away from her father and his new family as well as from her grandmother, with whom she had a close and loving relationship. How could Sally justify such radical separations for one she loved so much? How could she know that the move would not seriously damage her daughter? These questions haunted her. And no answers came.

To compound her own doubts and concerns, the people closest to her—her lover Peter, her parents, and friends, almost everyone apart from her daughter—condemned the idea and her for contemplating it. They implied that it would be a move of extreme selfishness that could only cause pain to all concerned. Peter, tormented by his own potential loss, suggested that such an act would be a betrayal of her destiny. Another person might have been able to dismiss such words with greater equanimity. But she had always had respect for his spiritual insights. He had displayed moments of accurate clairvoyance and perceptive vision when it came to the interests and natures of others. Moreover, their relationship had developed as a working partnership, one in which they had attempted, often successfully, to support each other's spiritual and psychological work. She knew no one else who had worked so hard and for so long, with such commitment and discipline, on his spiritual unfolding; and his insights into her, early in their relationship, had proved of considerable value and inspiration. So now to hear his words of judgment and condemnation, to hear him suggesting that what she called obeying the call of soul for its own becoming was in fact nothing but egocentricity, provoked and fed many of her own questions and doubts.

In the beginning she argued with him, foolishly trying to convince him of the validity of her inner voice, to allay his fears that it was the voice of evil rather than the voice of Self. But few can hear another's conscience, and least of all when their own perceptions are clouded and muddied by fear and pain.

But she was not completely alone with her convictions. For throughout this difficult time there was always one person who steadfastly and lovingly supported her decision: her analyst. This woman's consulting room continued to be a place of insight and nourishment amid a time of opposition, rejection, and condemnation; a warm place where she could speak out the pain and exhaustion of the conflict between the doubts and criticisms on one side and the still small voice of her dreams on the other. Together they worked to bring to consciousness that masculine part of her which resonated with the criticisms of others; to recognize and suffer his recriminations, his dislike of her doing anything which conflicted with the status quo, anything that she wanted; his approval of oughts and shoulds instead of individual life-giving needs. As this destructive inner figure became more conscious, she found it easier to live with the condemnations of those around her. She made her decision; sold her house, packed a few essential possessions, said goodbye, and holding the hand of her small, excited daughter, stepped onto the plane.

Selfishness is the most frequent criticism directed toward those who attempt to listen to, nourish, and cooperate with their own becoming. And certainly, from the outside, the process can look extremely selfish. Decisions appear to be made with little regard for the disruption and pain they may awaken in others, inviting such questions as "How can you be truly in touch with the necessity of your soul when it seems to cause so much pain? Surely you cannot be on the right path if it hurts those who love you." And often the only answer available does little to allay the doubts and suspicions. For the soul's response to such questions is that our primary responsibility is to our own unfolding, our own path to wholeness; that to serve this is the only way to serve others, and to betray it is to betray others. Moreover, it says that not doing or saying things which another may experience as hurtful is not necessarily the appropriate way to serve either one's own soul or that of the other. For sometimes it is necessary to make changes which another, emotionally dependent on the status quo, may find profoundly threatening and painful. And since there are no soul categories of selfish and unselfish acts, no laws or guidelines to follow at such times, the individual, alone with her conscience and the insights of the unconscious, has to decide which action to take; to decide, for instance, whether, under the circumstances, divorce would be an egocentric act or an act essential for soul-becoming. The observer, unless possessed of profound psychological and spiritual insight, sees only the divorce. He or she cannot judge whether it is in the interests of soul or solely in the interests of ego gratification, a flight from the opportunities for mutual unfolding inherent in many difficult marriages.

Selfishness is also important for the emerging ego consciousness, without which there can be no relationship to soul. The child and adolescent are rightly preoccupied with themselves, first with finding the appropriate nourishment and then with discovering their own interests and passions, and owning their rights as independent egos.

Selfishness, the primary importance of one's own I-ness and identity, is therefore essential at all periods of our unfolding. The only difference lies in what we experience as this I-ness, whether we identify it with our bodies and the interests of our ephemeral personalities, whether we are living within the parameters of an I–Thou relationship to Self, or whether we have realized our I as Self. In *The Dark Eye in Africa* (New York, 1955), Laurens van der Post describes one of his experiences with the bushmen which illustrates the psychic danger of loss of I-ness:

> Not long ago I came across a party of bushmen deep in the Kalahari. They had never seen white people before and as they mingled with my party in my camp I noticed a curious fact: they seemed compelled to do whatever we were doing. If we got up, they got up; if one of us moved, the bushman watching him would move too; if one of us eased his hat on his forehead, the bushman opposite him put up his hand and eased a hat that was not there. Now, we had a very distinguished man in our party, a fine-looking person with an impressive head and naturally dignified bearing. The leader of the bushmen gaily attached himself to this man as if it were his natural right, but soon a remarkable change set in in the little yellow man. A curious trancelike expression appeared on his face. Suddenly, just as the great man had given him a cigarette and lit one himself, I saw the little bushman imitating our great man, puffing when he puffed, removing the cigarette from his mouth when the other did in exactly the same way, and soon the yellow man had become so identified with the white man that he had no gestures of his own left. In some peculiar way he had become the quintessence of the great man and was almost more like a European than the European was himself. This went on for some while and then the bushman began to struggle with himself like someone in a nightmare. He looked wildly about him, cut the air between him and the European with two clenched, desperate hands, and in his way broke the spell. Then, realizing what had happened to him, he collapsed onto the sand shaking with laughter. But I noticed afterwards that the confiding manner with which he had attached himself to the white person had gone, that he gave the magnetic man only fearful sidelong glances and kept well away from him.
>
> (pp. 132–34)

It seems an inevitable law that when one person begins to listen inward, to search for his or her own truth and follow it, this has difficult repercussions for those closely connected to that person. Whether these are regarded as testimony to the selfishness of that individual depends in part on our view of pain. For if pain is considered bad, something to be avoided at all costs, then serving soul is likely to be equated with happiness, and the individual whose actions awaken pain in others equated with the devil. But if, on the other hand, the pain which occurs as a result of someone changing is seen not so much as something imposed on us by another but rather as an indication of our own emotional projection—evidence of the realms in which we have relied on another for our own feelings of security and emotional tranquility, for our own sense of wholeness—then the pain becomes an opportunity for our own growth. It becomes a possibility to withdraw the projection from the other person and find within ourselves that part of us which corresponds to the husband, daughter, or mother whose individual journey may in some way be taking them from us.

Traveling the way of soul, listening to and cooperating with its becoming, asks that we listen to and follow its laws even when, as often happens, these conflict with the accepted conventions and practices of culture and society. For an essential part of our own unfolding is finding and participating in our inner community, recognizing and obeying its own needs and laws. And as with all psychological wealth, the integration of our inner community depends, in part, on relinquishing attachment to and dependence on the ways and views of the outer one.

Tending soul requires patient and sensitive listening to inner needs and wants: resting when we need to rest, rather than when convention or habit dictates; respecting our desires for solitude even though others may consider it antisocial; weeping when there are tears to weep. . . . With each compassionate and understanding response to our needs, with each authentic expression of who we are, our capacity to recognize and respect our nature increases. And inasmuch as and only to the extent to which we can acknowledge, allow, and serve our own souls, we can acknowledge, allow, and serve the souls of others. For as a Chinese peasant said in response to a Western journalist's question about the meaning of Christianity: "It means loving oneself so that one can love others."

When we do not honor our own experience and needs, then our relationships to others tend to be characterized more by duty than by love—sometimes a noble duty, but more often one peppered with anger and resentment. Sally's years as a single parent provided her with many opportunities to recognize the difficult dynamic which occurs when a child's pain resonates with the unconscious wounded child within the parent.

One afternoon Sally looked up from her work to see Rachael turn into the garden from the street, her humped shoulders and heavy steps testimony to the end of a painful day at school. By the time Sally reached the front door her thoughts of the day's work had virtually vanished, leaving her free to give her daughter a long warm hug. Together they walked to the window seat and sat down in the late afternoon sun. Sinking her eleven-year-old head into Sally's lap, Rachael drank in the flow of love coming toward her. Soon she began to speak of her troubled day, of the children who left her out of their game, the teacher who mistook her feelings of incompetency for sullen noncooperation. Sally listened, not interrupting the story, not trying to fix the pain, to take it away, just hearing and receiving it. Part of her longed to protect her daughter from such trials, but for some time she had felt there were fewer and fewer areas in which this was either possible or appropriate, that her contribution as a mother lay in watching, listening, and supporting Rachael as she met and suffered the bumps and cuts life brought her, simply offering warm, nonjudgmental arms in which Rachael could let her tears fall, but not trying to remove the tears.

Sally stroked Rachael's soft, fair hair, idly running her fingers over the baby-fine fuzz of growth along the hairline. As she did this her mind wandered to a similar afternoon about six years earlier. Rachael had returned home from a birthday party in an intensely irritable mood. Everything Sally did or said only made it worse. Soon she was as irritated as her daughter. She longed for Rachael to stop crying, or at least to leave her alone. But the more she tried to quiet her cries the louder they became, until in desperation she put Rachael to bed, hoping she might cry herself to sleep. But the tears of unhappiness were now amplified by tears of anger at not receiving the comfort and understanding she needed. So instead of staying in bed, Rachael rampaged around the house, screaming. Sally felt her own aggression rising. She wanted to hit Rachael, anything to shut her up, to obliterate the sounds of her pain. For Rachael's screams seemed to be eating into her.

Calling on a long upbringing in self-control she resisted her aggressive desires and instead took Rachael in her arms, stroking her until she fell asleep. But her gestures were motivated more by duty and desperation than love. Once Rachael was asleep, Sally tiptoed out of the bedroom and went downstairs to her own room. Lying on her bed, exhausted by the drama, she began to reflect on what had happened. It was nothing new. There had been countless other incidents like this since Rachael was born. Moments when Rachael's cries of pain or needs had provoked anger from her rather than comfort or nourishment. But now, for the first time, she asked herself why Rachael's pain had this effect on her, why it irritated her so intensely. She listened again to the cries of the afternoon; felt how they seemed to penetrate her skin, fusing with herself, as though they were her cries, not Rachael's. Suddenly she realized that was true. They were her cries, the cries of her own bitterly unhappy inner child, the one who had always longed to be held and listened to, loved and supported through the seemingly endless childhood troubles, but whose pain had usually been met with no more than a brief hug and then some sensible advice about being brave and thinking about other things.

She began to cry, weeping the tears she had never been able to fully weep as a child, feeling the raw wounds, the coldness of no large arms to comfort her. She cried and cried, late into the night, reliving memory after painful memory—the moment when she had been frightened of the snakes in the garden and her mother had only been able to criticize her for forgetting in her fright to turn off the garden hose; the moment when she had been falsely accused of stealing buns; the moments when she was sick, and for a few days received her mother's warmth, but then the terrible coldness as that warmth was withdrawn and life was supposed to get back to normal.

As the memories and their long-buried pain returned to her that evening, surfacing from the graveyard of her soul, she discovered unfamiliar feelings of sympathy and compassion for this wounded and hungry little girl.

"Can we play a game?" Rachael's question brought her back to the sunny window seat. She looked at her and smiled. "Yes," she replied, "but first I need a few moments to myself. Why don't you get the game ready in the sitting room and I will join you soon."

Rachael left the room smiling, the unhappy day no more than a fading memory. Sally smiled too as she remembered with gratitude the Jungian analyst whose warmth, compassion, and understanding had prepared her for that evening six years ago when she recognized and suffered the wounds of her own childhood. Without that woman, she thought to herself, she might still hate the sound of her daughter's pain, might still try to get rid of it, deny it, fix it, anything to obliterate it from consciousness. And instead of a smiling, calm daughter in the sitting room, she would now have a raging or sullen one.

With the birth of Self, the process of following and cooperating with the soul acquires new depth. Instead of merely swimming with the river of our becoming, we become able, at moments, to experience its source and destination. At these moments we cease to experience ourselves as separate individuals confined within the boundaries of body and personality, or even as separate souls, and feel ourselves embraced and contained within a much larger whole. Warmed, enlivened, moistened, and enlightened by this whole, we know it both as our Self, the Self of every individual, and the Self of nature and spirit, of deepest earth and farthest star.

As we become accustomed to swimming with the current of our river and sensing its source, we can begin to recognize moments when we have cast ourselves up on its banks, out of touch with its life-giving waters. And by listening for the thoughts, feelings, or actions which, by conflicting with the river's nature and flow remove us from it, we can enable a transformation of the discordant energy so that our consciousness may once again unite with the flow of being and becoming.

Flowing with our river's journey requires continual change and adjustment. For an attitude, thought, or desire which once nourished and enlivened us does not necessarily continue to do so. Often the opposite occurs. Instead of unfolding, it begins, at a certain moment, to cramp and crystallize. To keep living, therefore, we have to keep dying, shedding outworn desires, conceptions, and attitudes, even outworn relationships and situations, so as to make space for new ones to be born. For, as Goethe wrote, "One who has not the capacity to die and be reborn is like an opaque shadow on this dark earth."

Those actions which accord with the river are those we want rather than those which we feel obliged to do, or fear not doing, or do out of habit or convention. But while this soul-wanting, this soul-hunger, is qualitatively no different from ego-oriented wants, like wanting to become President, to win Wimbledon, or to write a literary masterpiece, the object of the wants changes in the process of finding and entering our river.

From the island-oriented perspective of ego, caring about another's well-being or the well-being of the earth, for instance, may feel at best an inspiring ideal, at worst a somewhat onerous responsibility.

For everything beyond the ephemeral personality and body seems from this perspective to be other and outer, creating an either-or worldview in which feeding myself is felt to be distinct and often in conflict with feeding another.

Fortunately, perhaps, we do not always exclusively follow our ego desires prior to finding our river. Indeed, the contribution of collective morality, whether formulated by religious or social mores, lies in providing moral codes and attitudes to protect us from the anarchy which arises when the ego is allowed to reign unchecked. For until we have touched the waters of our river and discovered that they are of the same substance as the waters of another's river, even the waters of the universe, it is useful for there to be laws prohibiting murder, rape, incest, as well as social conventions encouraging us to take care of others and of the earth.

But once we have stepped into the river many of the collective codes of behavior and morality become increasingly superfluous and in some instances obstructive to our becoming, not because we discover a new license to do what we want irrespective of other people, but because, in recognizing another's essence as the same as our own, we begin to want to care for others, to nourish their unfolding as we nourish our own. As this happens a shift occurs in the focus of the individual journey. Months, maybe years, of introspective self-analysis and exploration leading deeper and deeper into our unique individuality, years of listening to our personal wounds, respecting our hungers and passions, spontaneously lead us to the wish to serve others. We discover the boundaries of our wants expanding to include the wants of others and the wants of the earth. Having received so much in the process of unveiling and holding our own hungers, we find a new want unveiling itself within our soul—the want to give.

But sometimes, as Sally discovered in the course of her analysis, we may want to give before our own gifts have had the time and space to ripen sufficiently. Such an impulse may be fed by a reluctance to contain the tension of the new psychic energies coming to consciousness and by residual problems with receiving, as well as by the authentic wish to pass on to others the fruits of the gifts we have received.

Sally had arrived early for her analytic session that day. Her analyst was finishing some cooking, so she showed Sally into the small, womblike consulting room and returned to the kitchen. Some spicy smells wafted along the dark corridor into the room, surrounding

Sally as she sat in the usual large, comfortable leather chair, with her back to the window so that her face was always slightly in the shadow. Idly she wondered who her analyst was having to dinner; who would be fortunate enough to be a friend of this quiet, insightful person. Briefly she imagined herself as one of the dinner guests, then rapidly dismissed the idea as she realized that she had nothing to give to such a gathering at this moment. The gifts of the last two years of intensive analytic work were still too new, too embryonic to be reflected over dinner or anywhere other than the quiet spaces of this room and her own house. The tiny bud of her Self had only recently revealed itself; its petals, only showing a hint of their color, were still too delicate to risk exposure to harsh winds or the midday sun.

But delicate though it was, Sally did not doubt the existence of this small bud of Self; could not, for its still joy was often accessible to her these days, almost any time she chose to turn toward it and leave behind the turbulence of her own emotions or the emotions of those around her. Like a small candle flame fed by an inexhaustible supply of wax, this embryonic Self burned in her core—a warm, safe place in an otherwise changing world. She felt it now as she sat in the leather chair, and gratitude welled up as she acknowledged, more consciously than before, the debt she owed to the woman cooking dinner, a debt which the considerable financial cost of analysis could never repay. In her gentle, insightful way, this woman had helped her find the priceless treasure, the pearl of great price. How could such a debt be repaid? How could she convey the extent of her gratitude? In the midst of such thoughts and the love they stirred, her analyst walked in, bringing with her a few more wafts of food.

So she repeated her question aloud: "How can I ever thank you?"

Her analyst looked at her for a moment, smiling. Then she said, "You may repay me by honoring your own wish to become a therapist, and thereby giving to others, in your way, what I have given to you."

Sally looked at her analyst, moved by the truth of her words and the unspoken acknowledgment between them that such a time had not yet arrived.

Although money alone rarely seems an adequate way of thanking for psychological and spiritual gifts, the issue of the relationship

between money and the work can play a useful role in the therapeutic relationship. Some therapists believe their work should be
paid for with a regular fee comparable to other professionals; some
feel that since each working relationship is unique, its financial
aspect should also be unique, reflecting the particular needs and
circumstances of patient and therapist; and still others, considering
that this kind of work should be done entirely for its own sake, free
from considerations of financial reward, choose to separate their
work as much as possible from payment by not charging a fee and
leaving it to the patient how much, what and when, or if at all he
or she will contribute.

Those who work in this last way are sometimes regarded by the
first group as being unrelated to the mundane world. Such a view
would be valid if the therapist's decision not to charge a set fee is
motivated by a dislike of earthly things, a form of spiritual pride. But
not if it is born from an understanding and respect for the interdependence of all being, from the knowledge that every true gift comes
not from the personality but from the Self, and therefore does not
need to be repaid to any particular giver, but can be repaid just as
well to any other human being. For as Jesus Christ, the great embodiment of Self, is recorded as having said, "Inasmuch as ye have
done it to the least of these my little brethren, ye have done it unto
me" (Matthew 25:40).

Inasmuch as the therapist enables Self to flow through her to
others, she will be nourished by the Self—not just psychologically
and spiritually but also materially, according to the same law of the
interdependence of all things and all levels of being—body, soul,
and spirit. In other words, those who practice their authentic work,
the work they came to earth to do, will attract the necessary material
support, provided they acknowledge their wants and do not obstruct
their fulfillment by doubt, suspicion, or denial. For the act of giving
to Self, at whatever level—physical, psychological or spiritual—
spontaneously creates the space within us to receive. And provided
the channel between our various bodies—spiritual, psychological,
and physical—has been opened by the recognition and healing of
obstructing wounds, we can receive everything we need, at every
level that we need it.

According to the Maori people of New Zealand, every gift carries
with it a spirit. If the recipient wants to avoid misfortune he or she
must find a way to pass on this spirit, by giving something back

either to the donor or to someone else. The Maori conception of giving acknowledges the relationship between flow and well-being, the interdependence of health and the continual moving on of energy, whether it be physical or psychological. When we hold on to objects, concepts, abilities, or feelings we dam life's spontaneous flow. The energy stagnates and eventually festers, damaging the one it once enlivened. Psychological miserliness is no less destructive, and perhaps more destructive, than material miserliness. Both lead to a cramping of the personality, an increasing isolation from the world, from people, and from the inexhaustible abundance of Self.

But authentic receiving and giving are rare. For neither can occur without the ability and willingness to find, allow, and feel our emptiness, our void; without relinquishing those things which perhaps once nourished but now simply constipate us; without surrendering those shields which keep out the pain but also keep out our becoming.

Receiving gifts, even those she genuinely liked, had always seemed to be somewhat marred by embarrassment for Sally. Even as a child, she had found the gift-exchanging rituals at Christmas often more of an ordeal than a delight. Not just, as she once thought, because of the formal, measured way in which these were organized in her family, but more, as became clear in the course of her analysis, because her wounds had made her reluctant to risk receiving the sentiment of the giver along with the gift. Long ago she had armored her heart so as to make sure that potentially painful words and actions could not touch her. And this armor, of course, also protected her from any love which might come her way.

Sometimes, when the analytic hour ended and Sally had picked up her dream journal and put on her coat, her analyst would hug her good-bye. The first time it happened she was surprised and grateful. And though on subsequent occasions the element of surprise diminished, the gratitude did not. For prior to meeting this woman, Sally had rarely been able to believe that a woman could care for her consistently, week after week, with no unpredictable periods of hostility or coldness. Though she did not need the hugs to tell her of the caring—for this was apparent in the eyes, the voice, and demeanor of her analyst—they did provide an added assurance, something she could not dismiss as merely professional compassion. They helped to melt her fears more effectively than any words.

But despite the gratitude she felt after a hug, it was months before she was able to enjoy them as they were happening. Quite unconsciously she protected herself from these moments of warm bodily contact by holding her dream journal against her heart as she was hugged: a shield against any unforeseen attack. She was unaware of this shield until the moment it dissolved. This happened one afternoon, seemingly no different from any other, except that when her analyst embraced her in the narrow, dimly lit hallway outside the consulting room, Sally spontaneously allowed herself to receive not only the arms but also the love coming with the arms. She felt her heart being pierced by warmth, and suddenly she knew what it meant to receive love, to relinquish now superfluous psychic defenses and let in its warmth and life.

As she drove home that afternoon, her heart felt raw and new, but also soft and full. Tears of melting dampened her cheeks as she negotiated London traffic. When she arrived at her house, Rachael, who had been watching from an upstairs window for the car to turn the corner, ran downstairs to greet her. As they hugged some of the love Sally had just allowed in flowed out to Rachael. And Sally felt no less full.

Fear of our buried wounds, fear of them being touched and perhaps painfully awoken into consciousness by another's actions, makes us cautious of authentic receiving. It is painful to begin to relinquish the attempts to control our environment, to censor our experience; painful to allow the wounds within our souls to surface into consciousness. But as this happens and our capacity for feeling and experiencing increases, unveiling the archetypal good mother, the friend, and the father as inner and eternal realities living at the core of our psychological wounds, the impulse to censor the outer environment, to protect ourselves against unforeseen psychic attacks, cruel remarks, or loss of friendship diminishes. And our ability and willingness to receive, both physically and psychologically, increases, not only because we are less dependent on the thoughts and actions of others for our own sense of self-worth, less vulnerable to outer attacks once we have tended our inner sensitivities and wounds, but also because we have begun to discover the possibilities for becoming in all that comes toward us, whether by way of pain or joy.

While we can find our capacity for receiving prior to the birth of Self, authentic giving before this moment is less available. Of course the ego personality can learn to give, choose to withstand the feelings of emptiness, the sacrifice of impoverishing itself for another; it can even feel the joy of enriching others, sharing their joy. But there always remains a sense of having to choose between my richness or another's, between selfishness or unselfishness. Only the giving which comes from the Self—as in meditation, in deep love, or after the inner realization of Self—is a giving which does not feel like depletion or sacrifice but rather as a flowing out of psychic or physical wealth from an inexhaustible well. At such moments we find, for the first time, the inseparability of giving and receiving. Inasmuch as we give, we receive. And the more we give the more we are able to receive. For the act of giving itself opens up within us a wider and larger channel for receiving from others, from nature as well as from the psychological and spiritual realms.

The love which flows from this well of Self is qualitatively distinct from emotional or physical love. It is complete in itself, neither needing nor asking anything from the other. It is the love of Shakespeare's sonnet:

> *. . . Love is not love*
> *Which alters when it alteration finds,*
> *Or bends with the remover to remove:*
> *O, no! it is an ever-fixed mark,*
> *That looks on tempests and is never shaken;*
> *It is the star to every wand'ring bark,*
> *Whose worth's unknown, although his height*
> * be taken.*
> *Love's not Time's fool, though rosy lips and*
> * cheeks*
> *Within his bending sickle's compass come;*
> *Love alters not with his brief hours and*
> * weeks,*
> *But bears it out even to the edge of doom.*

Until we experience this unconditional love we may confuse it with the desire for love, often expressed as projection: those moments when we are in love with someone else, when we say, "I love you," meaning "I want you." The unconditional love of Self is also sometimes confused with indiscriminating approval, whereas, on the contrary, this love creates a greater capacity for discernment and discrimination than is possible when the mirror of our soul is obscured by the confusion of our own longings. It gives us the assurance to honor our likes and dislikes, to stand beside those things we value and to turn away from those we do not, regardless of how others, even those we love, may respond to us. It disentangles us from others and thereby enables us to love them more.

Sally first became conscious of the difference between love and attachment in relation to Rachael.

"Can we go to the park to try out my new roller skates?" Rachael asked, as Sally walked into the kitchen carrying two bulging baskets of food from the supermarket. She put them down on the table and looked at Rachael's excited face. Then she looked out of the window at the heavy grey sky. Its weight seemed to increase her own weight, to amplify the exhaustion which had lamed her all day. She turned back to Rachael, feeling the familiar phrase rising in her throat: "Not today, perhaps tomorrow." But when she saw Rachael's eager face again, she heard herself saying instead, "All right, but not for long. I have to get back to do some work."

The park was no more than a five-minute walk from their house. But it took longer today, since Rachael insisted on skating from the front door. She bumped her way over the uneven, wet pavement, falling down, getting up, dismayed by the unexpected realization that she had apparently not been born a perfect skater. Negotiating the steep flight of steps up to the bridge over the railway line which bordered the park was a particularly tricky enterprise. She had to sidestep her way up the slippery concrete, holding tightly to the rail on the one side and to Sally on the other. By the time they finally reached the smooth tarmac path which led past the children's playground on the right and on toward the ponds and tennis courts, Rachael was beginning to feel she was an accomplished skater. She let go of Sally's hand and launched forth on her own, a small figure in a light blue anorak beneath the grey afternoon sky. Sally walked behind, thinking about the paper she was writing, about her lover who hadn't called her that day, about dinner. . . .

Sometimes she left such disjointed musings for a moment to glance at the worn grass beside the path, the mass of dog droppings, the tree bravely withstanding the polluted air, or Rachael skating on in front, and then returned to her musings. But one time, as she looked out from her world, her eyes were drawn to Rachael's blue anorak, and this time they stayed there, arrested by her love spontaneously pouring toward the skating figure. There was no emotion in this love, no longings to embrace or be embraced by Rachael; no images of who she would like her to be; no need or desire for anything from her; and no need to give anything to her—just an outpouring of silent and quiet love, a flow of warmth from her eyes and heart toward a human being who, only incidentally, it seemed, happened to be her daughter.

The unconditional love which is the hallmark of the Self is only accessible when we are, for a moment, in touch with our own wholeness, our fulfillment and completion. When two people fall in love they fall into the being of Self. But this flame is a fragile one, dependent for its life on harmony between the two people. The slightest disharmony snuffs it out.

It is rare that we stay in love for long. Our ideal projections onto the other crumble in the light of ordinary life: the woman finds it difficult to maintain her beauty throughout a busy day at the office or while washing the kitchen floor, the man his charisma while mowing the lawn or changing diapers. The perfect union of the ideal masculine with the ideal feminine leaves no space for our jagged, awkward, and raw becoming, for our shadows as well as our radiance, no space for human imperfection. Perhaps fortunately so. For as individuals we are more than just embodiments of the masculine and feminine. We contain the seeds of wholeness. So to the extent that we fall into love by way of another, we are inhibited from falling into love by way of our own soul.

But while it lasts, the state of being "in love" by way of another is not an illusion. It is a nourishing and inspiring opportunity, a fall into the source of love, into Self. Not my self or your self, not even our self, but the Self which is simultaneously you and I. Regardless of how it happens, whether in a brief meditative flash or through the image of our complementary nature mirrored back to us by way of another, such moments of being "in love" are the food of our becoming. For every touch of Self strengthens the soul's capacity to receive its Self. Moreover, behind the ephemeral condition of being "in love" may lie a possibility for authentic loving, for genuine caring and closeness with another human being.

The only illusion in the "in love" experience, apart from the discrepancies between our image of the beloved and his or her real nature, is the sense that the bliss could continue indefinitely—the fact that we do not recognize it as an inspiring and probably ephemeral glimpse into a state of being which is available to each of us, independent of another—a state of being as accessible in a crowded subway, at the funeral of the loved one, or alone in a Himalayan cave, as in the act of making love.

Since it is only possible to be in love with another by way of projection, it is a state often at odds with loving, a state of dependency which, as history testifies, can spawn the most hideous as well as the most inspired acts. Never is it a condition which allows us to stand calmly in the presence of another with love, irrespective of whether that person is fulfilling our desires or our fantasies of relationship. For when we say, "I love you"—really meaning "I am in love with you"—we are more likely to be saying something like "Our relationship gives me the experience of love," or "I am in the presence of love," rather than "I am able to love you; to allow at least a little of the unconditional love of Self to warm and support you in your journey of unfolding."

As the synthesis and source of the two poles of our being, body and spirit, the love that is Self is a healing force, bringing wholeness and health to previously one-sided, polarized conditions. A woman, for instance, who has oscillated between the roles of nun and whore in her relationships with men, alternately expressing the energy of spirit and the instinctive, undifferentiated energy of body, can now integrate the two poles by way of the source of all polarities, the Self. She can make love without losing her spirituality, and enjoy the spirit without relinquishing its reflection in body. From such a person comes an energy which heals and makes whole, restoring balance and health to herself and others, as well as to the earth.

As that which connects the opposites, the realization of Self allows for inner peace instead of war. It is a peace which enables us to recognize the different natures and destinies not only of other individuals but also of nations, and to respect and enjoy these differences while appreciating the interweaving oneness which underlies them. It shows us that the major contribution each of us can make to creating world peace is to recognize and heal the war within us. As this occurs, our own lives and those of others as well as the life of nature begins to flourish, enlivened as much by our being as by our doing.

Carl Jung was fond of illustrating this truth by telling the traditional Chinese tale of the Rainmaker, which I have paraphrased here:

For a long time no rain had fallen on the village. The streams had disappeared; even the riverbed was dry. The last of the grain from the public store had been distributed, and this year's crops, no longer able to stand, drooped toward the cracked earth. Once more the Chinese villagers prayed to the local deities, and once more they performed the customary rituals and sacrifices. But still no rain fell. And none seemed likely. The sun did not appear eager to relinquish its power over the earth and allow the arrival of moist, life-bringing clouds.

In despair the people decided to send someone to ask the renowned Rainmaker to come to their village. Since he lived many days' journey away, the villagers had plenty of time to discuss how to welcome and honor their exalted guest, should he choose to come. They gathered together what few treasured possessions and remnants of food still remained.

But when, at last, the Rainmaker arrived, he refused everything. He wanted neither food nor treasures, nothing except a quiet cave in which to be in solitude. Somewhat perplexed, but eager to grant his wishes, however menial, the villagers led the Rainmaker to a small cave at the edge of the village and left him there.

For three days no sound came from the cave, and no one saw their strange guest. The people began to worry and whisper among themselves. But in the evening of the third day, the Rainmaker emerged. As he walked toward the anxious and expectant villagers, dark clouds began to gather and obscure the sun, a gentle breeze moved over the land, and it rained.

The amazed villagers asked the Rainmaker what he had done to make the rain come.

"I withdrew into my soul," He replied. "I allowed my Self to be, and I waited."

Chapter Five

FIRE OF SELF

"You must be consumed by your center. You must pick up the reins of that sacred horse called spirit fire and balance between the positive and the negative forces. As a warrioress, as a woman of power, you must mount the central fire like a horse and unite with the infinite universe. . . . the Great Spirit and the Great Mother have not given you life that you would be alone. To know that you are truly alone is the first step on a long journey to self-discovery on the path to power. The next step is to learn that you are linked with the universe, that you live in all the lodges of the universe. Life flowers and nourishes itself from within. Beingness has realized itself within you. . . . You think that your life has nothing to do with any other life. This is the self-council. In self-council you must separate and become responsible for your own power. This process cuts cords that bleed your much-needed energy. When that is accomplished, a realization occurs. You open to the grand council and the great council fires within. You begin to understand that the galaxies, the mother stars, all existence, in fact, awakens within your own being. In a sense you *are* all existence. You are the womb from which the stars are born. All life is your firstborn child. The trees, the flowers, and all the creatures of earth have their rootedness in your special being. It does not seem so, but it has always been that way. To know these things, the central council fires of your personal experience must be ignited, and you must warm your hands on your own inner-spirit flame."

(Lynn V. Andrews, *Star Woman*, New York, 1986, pp. 239, 243–44)

The birth of Self is the conscious realization of our individual and cosmic wholeness and fulfillment. It awakens us to our rootedness in peace and joy by expanding our scale of being beyond the limitations which generate emotional desires and suffering. But like all newly-born things, the Self is a small and fragile spark at its birth, easily drowned by the clamor and turbulence of still unconscious and therefore unintegrated fragments of our being, by our inability to remain continually in tune with its refined frequencies. Its tender, tenuous presence needs time and nourishment if it is to find the necessary strength and maturity to become a permanent conscious reality.

The fulfillment which characterizes the experience of Self is due to its nature as the bridge and unity of the different poles of our being, the vertical pole of heaven and earth, spirit and matter, and the horizontal one of the masculine and feminine. As the midpoint and the totality of this cross, Self embraces and creates our being. In facilitating a conscious interchange between these poles, it enables the opposites to relate to each other. And as they relate, whether physically in sex or psychologically as the union of the masculine and feminine within the vessel of soul, there is creation.

The creative work of Self occurs, like much creation, by way of destruction. The spark ignited by the meeting of the opposites burns into the soul, purifying and refining all the energy made available to it; transforming the different psychic substances into its own essence as they are gathered and integrated into consciousness; absorbing the different energy levels into its own. And as soul is thereby transformed, it inevitably and unavoidably refines and transforms its earthly manifestation—the body.

This process of physical transformation can be, as Sally discovered, an uncomfortable and disquieting experience; her introduction to it was constellated by a dream:

A tall, golden-haired man approached her during the fish course of a banquet. She was immediately attracted to his combination of strength and refinement, nobility and gentleness. Beckoning her to follow him, he led her to the crumbling doorway leading into the earth at the foot of a large, barnlike building. As soon as her eyes became accustomed to the darkness, she found herself amid earthen corridors, filled with ancient ghostlike shapes and beings. Somewhat alarmed, she stayed close to her confident guide as they descended further and further into the ancient dark until all sounds and moving shapes were left behind.

Finally they arrived at a well-lit underground house. At one end of the house a Kabbalistic meeting was taking place at a round table. Her guide indicated that before she could join this group she must meet Moses, who was at the other end of the house. The meeting was brief, more acknowledgment than encounter. And then she was taken to the round table.

She was the last member of the group to arrive. The others had obviously been there for some time and were already involved in the work. The task seemed to be for each person to find and perform his or her "hand dance." She looked at the other people, wondering what a hand dance was and how she was supposed to find it. As no one offered her any advice, she began by trying to copy the hand movements of the person sitting next to her. But that soon proved to be impossible. They were too fast and complicated and had no apparent pattern or rhythm. So she gave up and sat for a while, somewhat bemused by the situation. Then she realized that she had to discover her own unique hand dance.

As she reflected on the dream the next day, feeling the awesomeness of the round-table meeting and the imperative of finding her own hand dance, she was reminded of the Sufi dervishes, who used dancing as a way of becoming one with God. And this association helped her to understand a little of the meeting with the dream Moses. For in leading the Israelites out of the land of bondage, Moses led them to the threshold of the Self, the mountains overlooking the promised land. But he died before he was able to take them into that land of milk and honey which, in Kabbalistic language, is known as the land of the I AM THAT I AM, a symbol of our union with God.

Psychologically, therefore, Moses symbolizes the one within us who can free the soul from its bondage to the desires and limitations of the body, free it from identifications with and attachments to the ephemeral, the materialism of the last days of Egypt, so that we can glimpse the promised land, the Self, and thereby find the psychological freedom to relate to both body and spirit rather than be enslaved by either. The dream reflected the fact that, though she had met her Moses and sufficiently dis-identified with her ephemeral form to glimpse the promised land, she could not enter without finding her own "hand dance."

Since the dream provided no indication as to how she might do this, Sally decided to contemplate her hands for a while. She had always enjoyed her hands. Their long, fine bones pleased her aesthetic sense. So she started to move them, to play with them, and to imagine them performing a dance. Slowly they acquired a will of their own. She stopped choosing what to do with them, and began watching, sensing what they wanted to do, enjoying the abundant variety of hand gestures which became possible once her hands were allowed to move and interact spontaneously.

After a while her hands stopped moving, giving her time to ponder the meaning and value of hands, their capacity to give and to receive, to touch and to hold; time to reflect on how she used her hands, how she related to others and to the earth, how and what she gave and received.

Before long she found herself eager to return to the hand-play, to the pleasure of its spontaneous movements. But this time she was more aware of the feel of her hands touching and being touched by the air than of their particular movements. For her the palms suddenly felt acutely sensitive, as though they were being rained upon by tiny sparks. She looked at them, expecting to see some sign of this surprising sensation. But they looked the same as always, with not the smallest visible reflection of the "burning" which felt as though it was consuming her flesh. She realized that "burning" was only an approximate adjective for the uncomfortable, sometimes painful sensation. There was no feeling of heat, yet the image was unmistakably that of her body, and particularly her palms, being refined, purified, and transformed by a shower of radiant liquid light.

She continued to sit crosslegged and attend to this novel phenomenon. The light in the room was dim, veiled by the tall, leafy lime trees which grew in the small patch of earth between her house and the city street; this morning the light was even further obscured by the charcoal grey clouds of an approaching storm. The house was silent. Rachael was at school. So it seemed she had ample time to explore this new experience. After the initial amazement and excitement, she felt a certain awe arising in her for the origin of these tiny sparks, for the invisible but palpable white light which appeared to be their source. Though it had arrived without any conscious invitation, she now welcomed it, gladly cooperating with its touch by stilling her thoughts and feelings so that its energy was not deflected.

The next time she looked outside the window, the dark clouds had passed, allowing a dappled light to filter through the leaves. Feeling hungry, she got up and moved toward the kitchen. Instantly her interest in the burning changed to alarm. For each contact with the floor was painful to her feet. And as she grasped the door handle she found that the palms of her hands hurt in the same way. Both, it seemed, had become so sensitized by the fire that anything more solid than air seemed to scrape and rasp against them. She sat down on the sofa, horrified at what was happening to her. The fire, which only a few minutes ago seemed a benevolent and purifying agent, now felt like an enemy, threatening to incapacitate her. How could she look after Rachael, drive the car, go to supermarkets if every step and touch made her wince?

She got up again, determined to discover just how crippled she had become. Tiptoeing to the kitchen, she opened the refrigerator door with the ends of her fingers and began to prepare some granola and fruit. She ate, taking care not to allow the spoon handle to bump against the palm of her hand. Then she tiptoed upstairs to the bedroom and lay down.

She wanted to telephone her new American analyst to ask him if he was familiar with this experience, what it meant, how long it might last. But she was too cautious of imposing herself, still too insecure to risk asking for unpaid minutes. She rationalized her fear by imagining what it might be like to be an analyst and have every analysand calling each time something strange occurred. She imagined the burden, the exhaustion. In the midst of these imaginings she must have fallen asleep, for the next thing she heard was the sound of the front door being opened and Rachael running upstairs. Without thinking Sally got up off the bed and walked quickly to greet her. As usual Rachael was hungry, having eaten little of the school lunch. So Sally made her some hot toast and butter and listened to the day's events at school, summarized by Rachael in between mouthfuls. It was only when Rachael left the kitchen for a moment to go to the bathroom that Sally remembered the burning. It had gone, and it did not return that evening. But the next day, after she had driven Rachael to school and was sitting in her meditative position again beneath the window, it was back, as powerfully as the morning before.

As the days passed Sally realized that the burning had come to stay, that it was not an ephemeral event but an integral part of her life. Its coming and going within each day seemed to vary, as did its intensity. The only constant seemed to be its presence during meditation, and its disappearance or considerable weakening whenever Sally was actively involved in caring for Rachael or doing the most basic necessities, such as buying food. The rest of the time she either had to stop what she was doing and allow the fire to burn, or find ways of withstanding the sensitivity it created. The regularity with which it diminished whenever she was caring for Rachael gave Sally a certain respect for its work. She began to regard it as a benevolent and wise guide, to feel that it was sorting out the essential from the inessential activities in her life and telling her that, though she could continue the inessential, it might be wise to relinquish them and cooperate with its work.

Perhaps it was fortunate that Sally did not know then what a lengthy companionship she had embarked upon. She could not see the seven years of burning stretching ahead.

Fire expresses the relationship and wholeness inherent in all duality. For its being depends on the interplay of the two poles of existence, matter and air. Deprived of one or the other, it dies. Thus it has been widely regarded as an image of God: Agni, the Vedic god of fire, is considered the son of Heaven and Earth, and, as such, as the messenger between the gods and humanity; in the *Bhagavad Gita* the Lord Krishna says, "I am the fire residing in the bodies of all things which have life"; in the Medicine Lodge of Native Americans, fire is the sacred dwelling place of the great spirit as well as the intermediary between gods and men; in the Bible, God is described as a "consuming fire" (Deut. 4:24). He announces His presence to Moses as a burning bush, and in the New Testament the Holy Spirit descends on the disciples' heads as flames of fire.

Apart from visible earthly flames, fire also manifests itself in various ways at every other level of existence, becoming increasingly refined as it ascends from earthly to spiritual planes. It lives as the heat of sexual passion in the body; as anger, desire, and romantic love in the emotions; as unconditional love in the core of soul; and as radiant light and insight in the spirit.

Fire is the agent of transformation, the means by which matter returns to spirit. Water, for example, can change into steam and evaporate as air; and candle wax melts as it dissipates into warmth and light. But if the water is drunk before it reaches the requisite temperature, or the candle wax used before it is touched by the flame, there is no transformation. The wax and water merely move horizontally into another mode of being, their essential nature unchanged. And the same is true of psychological transformation. In order for psychic energy to find itself at a new and more refined level of being, it needs to be contained—held rather than dissipated through physical, emotional, or intellectual events. The tension and heat need to be allowed to increase without being spilled, so that the necessary temperature for transformation may be reached.

One of the ways in which soul accumulates energy and thereby expands is, as we have seen, through the slow, often painful work of integrating hitherto repressed or unconscious psychic contents. This work of meeting and making love with our inner masculine and feminine qualities, withdrawing our projections without necessarily acting them out by way of romantic affairs, enables psychic energy to accumulate, and, in time, become ready for transformation.

Sexual energy can be seen as an example of the potential for transformation inherent in all energy. The instinctive response to the accumulation of sexual excitement, as with other forms of tension, is to seek release. And since sexual release in orgasm is a pleasurable experience, there might appear to be little reason to inhibit it. But psychological becoming does not always move by way of the easy and pleasurable. The medieval alchemists called it the *opus contra naturam* ("the work against nature"). If sexual energy is gathered and held, either as it spontaneously arises within us as a result of erotic thoughts or feelings, or in the act of lovemaking, it will, with our cooperation, reach a certain level of intensity and then, like water turning into steam, transform itself into heart feelings.

In the Tantric tradition of India, sexual energy is understood within the context of the raising of the Kundalini. Although at the time of her dream Sally was unfamiliar with the details of Kundalini Yoga, she later discovered that they contained a striking correspondence to her dream and the transformation by "fire" which it initiated. For Tantric texts teach how to descend into the pit of our being, the chakra at the base of the spine, where the Kundalini snake lies coiled in sleep, to awaken it into consciousness and, with divine cooperation, to invite it to ascend the spine, passing through the higher and higher energy frequencies of the different chakras until it reaches the crown chakra and, resolving duality, unites with Shiva, the pure consciousness pervading the whole universe. The Kundalini energy, known as Shakti, is regarded as the female energy existing in latent form, not only in each human being but in each atom of the universe, while the Shiva energy is regarded as male. In the beginning of each moment of creation, according to Tantric tradition, the one cosmic consciousness divides into these two poles, and the duality which characterizes our earthly existence comes into being.

Kundalini Yoga teaches certain hand movements, known as mudras. These are a ritualized body language designed to express the individual's surrender and invocation to the deity to enter and invite the coiled snake energy to begin its journey of ascent. These mudras correspond to the hand dance Sally was asked to find at the Kabbalistic round-table meeting in her dream. The sacred nature of this process of transformation depends on the sacrifice of all personal desires, attitudes, and considerations. For the two poles of our being cannot reconnect with each other as Self, our cosmic human being, if we are deflecting the energy to create a personal world of thoughts and feelings.

After reading about Tantric Yoga, Sally was able to understand somewhat better why her own "burning" process seemed to allow her to do only those things which were essential for her own well-being and that of others, but seemed to incapacitate her when she tried to do many of the things with which she had once filled her days; she now understood why she could drive Rachael to school or cook her dinner, but not continue the book she was writing or attend parties without considerable discomfort.

The raising of the Kundalini cannot occur without consciously relinquishing identification of the accumulating energy with any of the particular chakras, or levels of energy, through which it has to pass on its ascent from body to spirit. The first act of dis-identification has to take place in relation to the genitals. It is necessary to relinquish the idea that sexual tension can only be released sexually, and next to invite this energy to ascend the spinal column to the heart. The process requires the ability to hold the energy, withstanding the desire for physical release, and to simultaneously relax the body so that the concentration of heat and blood can leave the genitals and travel up as a warm glow, first into the solar plexus, vitalizing and heating the whole stomach, and then into the heart where it finds a new form as soul warmth, and love. This work of relaxing and disidentifying the energy from any particular location, physical or psychic, can then be continued on beyond the heart to the crown of the head, where heart warmth transforms itself into radiant light and spiritual wisdom.

Each stage of transformation depends on the energy being treasured rather than denied, so that none of it is lost along the way; so that sexual passion, for example, is not repressed but given the opportunity to find greater strength and refinement as love. If the process is attempted by way of denial rather than respectful holding, the sexual energy will get locked in the body, leading to its frustration and stagnation, and possible physical disease. If the pathway between body and soul is blocked by denial, the body will be unable to receive and express psychological energy, and the soul will be correspondingly depleted of the vital forces of body and earth. Likewise, if feelings and emotions are denied, the light of the spirit may be perceived, but it will be devoid of the warmth and life of soul. For when there is repression there can be no transformation, merely a perpetuation of duality—body or heart, heart or spirit. So it is essential to live fully the possibilities and passions of the body and heart to enjoy their pleasures and excitement before beginning the alchemical work. For if any part of us has not been sufficiently owned, inhabited, and appreciated for what it is, the alchemical work will be without its essential ingredients, without the primal matter of Self, and we will be sadly lifeless beings, unrelated, unnourished, and unappreciative of the earth on which we live.

The alchemical work, the *opus contra naturam,* transforms the nature of sexual relations. By way of it we cease to be victims of our sexual and emotional desires and become, instead, conscious participators in sexuality, enjoying, for the first time, a degree of freedom and choice as to whether to allow our energy to express itself physically in sex, psychically in love, or spiritually in serene and joyful radiance. Once this freedom is available celibacy ceases to be exclusively for those in monastic orders, bound by strict rules and moral codes, or for those frightened by and therefore alienated from their bodies and the powerful energies of this earth, and becomes instead a viable choice for each of us, a mode of being which is appropriate to certain periods of our lives. It becomes something which neither deprives us of relationship to body and earth nor diminishes our capacity to love others, but which, on the contrary, may enhance both forms of experience. For as our ability to receive and to give love is freed from its projection onto body, and our psychic needs and hungers are no longer lived out by way of physical needs and hungers, we become increasingly able to see, accept, and enjoy our own natures, those of others, and the earth for what they are, unencumbered by our psychic projections onto them.

The transformation of energy is a process readily reflected in dreams. As an image begins to rise into consciousness it often appears in its least refined form. But as it is met and welcomed into consciousness, accepted in its rugged, primitive, even ugly and wounded manifestation, not only the conscious mind but (as we saw in the story of Beauty and the Beast) the image itself is transformed. The young *femme fatale* with her voluptuous breasts and hips, her thick dark hair and large lips may become the slim, gentle beauty; the hulky animal hunter becomes the noble hunter of wisdom; and the wounded tomcats become strong, noble young men.

Cooperating with this transformative work is not comfortable, however. For individual consciousness becomes accustomed to living within certain parameters, certain acceptable fluctuations of energy reflecting familiar mental, emotional, and physical conditions. These parameters change dramatically once we cease to dissipate our energy through needless chatter, uncreative orgasm, and other forms of unnecessary activity, and begin consciously to gather and contain it, allowing it to accumulate the heat which spontaneously raises and transforms it into progressively finer frequencies.

But this process of transformation can feel distinctly awkward, even frightening, its strangeness sometimes difficult to endure. For as the vibrations of psychic energy are raised, the dross refined and purified, and body and soul are flooded by greater power and light, they have to relinquish their old modes of being. This requires a continual process of shedding and sacrifice. Discovering how to cooperate with rather than obstruct this work, as Sally discovered, is not easy. We can read about it. But no amount of words can adequately prepare us for the experience itself or teach us how to relate to it. In the end, as usual, it is the experience itself which is our most reliable teacher, provided we listen to it attentively.

Sally had agreed to have lunch with Sarah, a woman she had met recently, and, knowing the care and time Sarah would have put into preparing the food, she did not want to cancel an hour before she was due to arrive, even though the "burning" had been more intense than usual for the last few days.

So she gathered her coat and set off for the subway. As she struggled through the crowds and toxic fumes of city life she became aware of a new and very uncomfortable sensation accompanying the "burning." It felt as though she were becoming a pressure cooker. For although she was already filled with more energy than she felt she could contain, it seemed that yet more psychic substance was being stuffed into her. As she sat on a corner seat next to a businessman reading a financial journal, she glanced down at her body to check if it showed any signs of this extraordinary pressure. But she could see nothing. Straining to see around the shoulders of a large woman on the opposite seat, she examined her face in the window glass. But it too looked relatively normal, perhaps more tired than usual, but nothing exceptional. Yet by the time the subway reached her stop the tension had increased considerably.

Like a cripple, she struggled along the busy shopping street, trying to find a way to minimize the impact of the sidewalk on her painfully sensitive soles, while hoping that her body would not explode, spilling its contents over the road, in a final attempt to release the pressure.

Lunch was difficult. The "burning" and now this new experience of her skin having to contain more energy than it was used to containing made Sally feel somewhat freakish. She did not understand what it meant, and did not feel comfortable enough with Sarah, a much older woman whom she did not know well, to expose her pain and confusion. So she attempted to participate in discussions about Jung and psychology while the pressure continued to mount, seemingly indifferent to the difficulties it was creating for her. When she finally got home that afternoon she went to bed, relieved that whatever awful event was about to happen could happen in privacy.

The pressure at the top of her head continued to increase. At first she just lay there, glad to be home. But then she asked herself if there was anything she could do to assist the process. For she was now sufficiently familiar with the ways of soul-unfolding to know that such psychic events need the cooperation of consciousness rather than struggle and obstruction. So she allowed herself to experience as deeply as possible the image of her skin being filled to the bursting point. As she did so the solution spontaneously revealed itself. She needed to let go of this old skin, slough it like a snake.

Until this realization, Sally had felt identified with her swollen psychological skin and so could not see any way to let it go. But lying on the bed, relating to the image, helped her to experience a separation between her being and its old psychic identity and now redundant parameters, and this allowed her to imagine the possibility of relinquishing it. The process felt somewhat like getting undressed. But instead of actively contorting the body to release it from a coat, she found the skin slipped off more easily if she relaxed and gently allowed the tension to dissolve.

When the skin had been completely sloughed off she found herself in a much larger space, one which easily contained the new influx of energy. The morning's discomfort ceased. She closed her eyes and rested, feeling huge and full.

As the fire of Self becomes conscious, transforming the dross brought to the surface by humbling journeys into the psychological abodes of our demons, it brings physical and psychological trials reminiscent of medieval images of hell. Yet, as the following dream reflects, the "burning" pits of soul are essentially of the same substance as its heaven.

Sally's path led her to the brink of a chasm of fire, a vast crater of flames. As she stopped in terror, a quiet voice told her that she had to enter this hell and walk through. So she inched a little closer and ventured one toe over the edge. Instantly she felt her skin seared by the heat. She stepped back swiftly, wondering what to do. The voice indicated that she had to undergo certain psychological and spiritual processes to prepare her for the journey through the flames of hell.

The preparatory experiences took considerable time, but eventually she was ready. Pushing a large red box of Christmas chocolates before her, she walked into the crater and cautiously began to follow a winding path through the flames. Soon she was surrounded, above and below, by a sea of fire, furnace-hot, touching every part of her body. Yet she felt no heat and no pain. Though the fire embraced her completely, it burned nothing. As she reached hell's deepest place she found herself in the presence of God.

Until Sally had completed the necessary spiritual and psychological work, those parts of her being composed of energies coarser than the flames were burned by them. But once the work of purification and refining was complete, once the primitive, cruder, even demonic energies had been admitted into consciousness and transformed by the influx of the spirit, her soul was able to withstand hell's flames. Not because it had acquired an asbestos shield, but because it had relinquished all shields; because its nature had been sufficiently refined by the painful work of psychological exploration, acceptance, and compassion to have become indistinguishable from the "all-consuming fire" itself.

This relationship between God, or Self, as the fire of destruction and the fire of enlightenment was described in detail in the sixteenth century by the Spanish mystic Saint John of the Cross in his book *Living Flame of Love:*

Here it must be known that, before this Divine fire of love is introduced into the substance of the soul, and is united with it, by means of a purity and purgation which is perfect and complete, this flame is wounding the soul, and destroying and consuming in it the imperfections of its evil habits; and this is the operation of the Holy Spirit, wherein He prepares it for Divine union and the transformation of its substance in God through love. For the same fire of love which afterwards is united with the soul and glorifies it is that which aforetime assailed it in order to purge it; even as the fire that penetrates the log of wood is the same that first of all attacked and wounded it with its flame, cleansing and stripping it of its accidents of ugliness, until, by means of its heat, it had prepared it to such a degree that it could enter it and transform it into itself. In this operation the soul endures great suffering and experiences grievous afflictions in its spirit, which at times overflow into the senses, at which times this flame is very oppressive. For in this preparatory state of purgation the flame is not bright to it, but dark. Neither is it sweet to it, but grievous; for, although at times it kindles within it the heat of love, this is accompanied by torment and affliction. And it is not delectable to it, but arid; it brings it neither refreshment nor peace, but consumes and proves it; neither is it glorious to it, but rather it makes it miserable and bitter, by means of the spiritual light of self-knowledge which it sheds upon it, for God sends fire, as Jeremiah says, into its bones, and tries it by fire.

(trans. E. Allison Peers, New York, 1962, pp. 43–44)

The psychological and physical hell into which the transforming fire of Self casts us is born from the meeting of our coarser energies with the pure touch of the living light of Self, the spark of God. Psychologically the fire burns away the defenses between consciousness and the unconscious, diminishing previous capacities to dissociate or in other ways shield ourselves from the ugly and primitive aspects of our souls. Its work occurs, of course, from the beginning of the journey of psychological exploration. It is the inevitable result of shining the light of consciousness into the inner darkness. But as we become able to embrace the depths of body and instinct as well as receive the radiance of the spirit, and as the Self is born into consciousness, the fire ceases to be a spasmodic occurrence and becomes an increasingly regular and more apparent companion along the way, rapidly burning away the layers of darkness which have protected us from our souls, thereby intensifying and hastening the process of psychological and physical transformation.

One of the immediate psychological responses to this fiery touch is a feeling of shame at the sight of the ugly and egocentric attitudes and attributes which the flames have helped to awaken into consciousness. Such shame is one of the hallmarks of the fire's work, and it persists until the old energy constellations responsible for all ways of being and feeling incompatible with the nature of the Self have been thoroughly burned away. The experience is of something hard and encrusted being relinquished and dissolved. It hurts, but it also loosens and relaxes. With the completion of each phase of this process, as the pain ceases and the cruder energy is thoroughly consumed by the touch of the Self, we feel simultaneously emptier and freer, cleaner and more fluid. The waters of our being seem to acquire new depth and vitality.

The fire of Self is indeed an all-consuming God. For once it has come to life within the soul, it resolutely and unsparingly consumes all that is not of the same pure frequency as Itself. From the perspective of ego's attachment to the ephemeral and personal, to everything which might serve the interests of personal aggrandisement, comfort, security, and temporal happiness, this is a ruthless process. But from the perspective of the Self, the fire refines the vessels of our being, thereby increasing our capacity to reflect Its life and love into the world, through our bodies, through relationships, and through caring for the earth.

The psychological changes wrought by the "burning" do not take long to reflect themselves. Rapidly outworn psychological tastes, inclinations, desires, attitudes, concepts, and interests wither and die, revealing new ones, both more satisfying and more truthful. And as the fire consumes and transforms the soul, it in turn spontaneously transforms the body, forging it into a more fitting expression of itself. As this happens, physical tastes change: certain foods and liquids, most notably stimulants like coffee, tea, alcohol, and sugar, become less attractive and eventually repugnant, and spicy flavors often feel too harsh for the rapidly sensitized body. The direction is toward simpler and blander foods, alive and uncontaminated ones.

At the same time, a new sensitivity toward physical surroundings becomes apparent. Initially the capacity to tolerate the toxins and noise pollution of cities may diminish as the old protective veils of unconsciousness, together with the cruder psychological energies, are burned away and the capacity to live entirely within the invulnerable being of Self is not yet established. At this time the peaceful and life-imbuing forces of nature become increasingly necessary and appealing, as does solitude.

Before the intense work of the fire, the physical body enjoys a certain degree of autonomy and immunity relative to soul. It can withstand a considerable amount of psychological and physical abuse—toxic food, toxic environments, even toxic emotions and thoughts—before beginning to break down in disease. But as the unconscious protective veil between body and soul is progressively burned by the conscious penetration of the Self, the body becomes an increasingly sensitive barometer of soul with each negative feeling and thought, each turbulent emotion immediately reflected by phys- ical discomfort. And as physical functions become less automatic, individual responsibility for health increases. It rests with each of us to ensure that we live in such a way as to be immune from the emotional and environmental dis-eases which might, over time, re- flect themselves as physical disease.

Relieving every pain

Learning to recognize, accept, relate to, and assume responsibility for the new power born from the increased sensitivity of soul and body is a difficult process and, because of its strangeness, a fright- ening one. Sometimes the fire's work feels like a vicious cycle. For each new phase of burning sensitizes the body to a new degree, making it correspondingly more vulnerable to environmental and psychological toxins, which can only be cleansed and healed by inviting more of the Self to flow into the soul, more of its purity and power. And this in turn inevitably invites more burning. Keeping psychological pace with this process, therefore, demands constant vigilance and a willingness for continual change: the ability to listen for the reality of the present rather than assume that the ways of yesterday will be viable today; the recognition that living depends on dying.

Like a musical instrument, the soul and its physical form can express the symphonies of Self—the songs of God—only as sensi- tively as its own degree of delicacy and refinement permits. For just as a Stradivarius allows levels of a Bach violin sonata to be heard which cannot be heard on a beginner's violin, so a finely wrought soul allows more of God's voice to be amplified than one unrefined by spiritual and psychological work. However, in the same way that the greater refinement of the Stradivarius makes it more vulnerable to abuse, the greater refinement of body and soul make them more susceptible to psychological and physical discord.

Learning to keep in tune with the spiral of refinement, to respect it by continually relinquishing inappropriate attitudes, actions, feel- ings, and thoughts for those more in harmony with its flow, is so difficult that it is likely to occur only by way of much discomfort, loneliness, and precarious ill-health. For old ways of being and relating hang heavily upon us, held in place by the power of uncon- scious habit. Many of the changes required to keep pace with the increasing sensitivity require major adjustments in feeling and thinking.

However, to the extent that the "burning" makes the body more sensitive to disharmonious thoughts and feelings, it also makes it more sensitive to harmonious ones, those which accord with the Self. As a result, active participation in one's own physical and psychological healing—useful at all stages of consciousness—becomes increasingly productive. For the psychological sensitivity and compassion for body which are born from meeting and accepting our earthly nature can considerably enhance our perception of physical disease in its embryonic stages, before the symptoms have acquired too deep a hold, thereby permitting consciousness more time to cooperate with the body's healing process by creating harmonious images, thoughts, and feelings, by allowing the health and joy of Self increasingly to permeate the soul and heal—make whole—the body.

It is necessary to attend to and nurture the body throughout the journey of becoming, not only at times of visible sickness. For the suffering and stress which are likely to constitute inevitable steps of this way exact a heavy toll on it. To avoid this stress is often merely to postpone it. So while we unfold by way of it, relinquishing identifications and projections, both soul and body need to be regularly nourished and strengthened by the healing energy of the spirit. Jung wrote that "we do not become enlightened by imagining figures of light, but by making the darkness conscious." (C. G. Jung, *Psychological Reflections*, Princeton, 1970, p. 220.) He recognized the work of finding and accepting the darkness of one's own psychic and physical realities as the precondition of transformation. But in so doing, Jung perhaps betrayed one of his own finest principles—that soul can be understood not by an "either-or" perspective but rather by "either-or-and." For psychologically we become healed (whole) and therefore enlightened not only by making the darkness conscious but also by imagining figures of light. The radiance of the spirit which is invited into consciousness and received into soul through image, prayer, and meditative practices helps to protect us as we suffer our own dark nights of becoming. It helps to facilitate the process of psychological transformation, lifting consciousness to new plateaus from whose vantage point anxieties and concerns which once loomed large now diminish into insignificance.

At the end of the first phase of Sally's "burning" she dreamed she was in a burning house. Upstairs a child called Kabbalah was being born from the flames.

As the esoteric core of Judaism, Kabbalah is a rich and complex body of knowledge concerned with the being and becoming of individual and cosmos. The word itself means "to receive the truth." Thus Sally's dream reflects how her child of wisdom, her capacity to experience and know the truth, was being born from the work of the fire, from its burning away all attachments and identifications with ephemeral realities, along with all ego-oriented fears and obsessions which might prevent her from experiencing her soul as the chalice of Self.

Chapter Six

DYING

"Now thou art fast to the rock. Here must thou grow old, for even the Devil with all his wiles cannot carry thee away, never and nevermore shalt thou get down." . . .

.   .   .   .   .

The first day after the fisherman had left him with mocking words, and Gregor remained behind quite solitary, he stopped where he was, sat with his arms round his knees or knelt with clasped hands before God. . . . But the second day was only a few hours old when hunger and thirst let him no longer rest and almost without knowing or willing it, on all fours, because he could not take a step with his feet in irons, he began to creep and seek round his little platform.

In the middle, almost exactly, there was a little trough in the stone, and a whitish cloudy wetness filled it up to the margin, probably yesterday's rain, he thought, only quite strikingly cloudy and milky— welcome to him in any case as a drink, however and whencever unclean it might be, he was the last to make conditions . . . and on the next day Gregor strengthened himself with the sap, lapped it all up, warmed to the point of sleepiness; for during the night he had suffered much from cold and not known how to pull his scanty shirt to find cover in it. . . .

80

. . . The winter went by strangely fast and seemed to him altogether short, on the simple ground that he slept much and jumped over and disregarded time. He took notice again only when the light grew, the breezes blew milder, and a spring, which indeed altered nothing of the treeless and grassless nakedness of his rocky seat, being able only mildly to warm the stone, passed over into long-dayed summer-time, where the sun described her highest arc in heaven above the lake and if storm-clouds did not shroud it, streamed down powerfully on man and rock, often making the latter so hot that the former could scarce have borne it if his defensive skin had not already turned very horny and granular. . . .

Finally, in fifteen years he was not much bigger than a hedgehog, a prickly, bristly moss-grown nature-thing, whom no weather could affect, and whose shrunken members, the little arms and legs, even eye- and mouth-openings were hard to recognize. It knew time no more. The moon changed, the constellations revolved, they vanished from the sky, they came again. The nights, moonbright or gloomy and dripping, icy with storm or sultry and close, shortened or lengthened. Dawn came, early or late, greyer or redder, flamed up and died down again in brilliant crimson that mirrored itself in the region of the east. . . .

And amid all that the mossy creature, when it was not asleep, went its creeping way to the mother-breast and returned filled and a little slobbering to the verge where the penitent had once been set down. If by chance a boat in the lake had neared the remote rock, the boatmen would have observed nothing striking up there. If the fisherman down in the wasteland had taken a notion to make the trip again and look round for the tiresome fellow he had landed here—a moment would have convinced him that he was long since perished and decayed, what remained of him dried, evaporated, and washed away from the stone. . . .

. . . . .

That morning [Probus] had shared with fervour in the general prayers in the Church of the Apostles Philip and James near his palace. Now he might have fallen asleep in the sweet air of the sun-warmed laurels, for he had a dream-vision. . . .

Before him in the meadow clover stood a bleeding lamb and spoke to him. . . .

"Hearken to that which I must announce to thee. Habetis papam. A pope is chosen unto you.". . .

"Let me learn: what is his name?"

"Gregorius," replied the Lamb. . . .

"Up, Probus! Seek him from land to land in Christendom and let no travail of the journey rue thee, let it lead thee now high over barren mountain heights, now across raging torrents. On a savage rock sits the Chosen One quite alone for full seventeen years. Seek and fetch him, for to him belongs the throne."

(Thomas Mann, *The Holy Sinner*, trans. H. T. Lowe-Porter, New York, 1959, pp. 256ff.)

Becoming depends on dying. The fire of Self expands and intensifies by consuming and absorbing everything it touches. But it can only touch those parts of soul accessible to consciousness. For consciousness functions like a valve in the neck of an egg timer. It has the power to deny, repress, and dissociate itself from psychic energy, both that which is locked up in personal wounds and ugly shadow qualities and that living as archetypal human qualities behind and within the personal and the particular. And this power of individual consciousness to close the gates to fields of Self operates as effectively in regard to the transcendent, formless light and wisdom of the spirit as it does to the emotional, instinctual depths of body and earth.

Although with the birth of Self both gates of consciousness open, allowing for the first time a regular interplay within the soul of spiritual and earthly energies, in the beginning the impact of this flow tends to be relatively weak. Many dimensions of spiritual and earthly nature remain untouched, unintegrated into consciousness. Many actions, thoughts, and feelings continue to occur without relation to the harmonious and joyous flow of Self. But each time that consciousness through patient, receptive, and attentive work integrates a new field of soul, this energy becomes vulnerable to the transforming fire of Self. Like dross coming to the surface, the explorer of the dark, unknown depths of being raises the coarse, ugly, and deformed energies into the light, where they may be transformed and consumed by the flames of Self, dying in their previous forms and finding new life within the eternal being of our divinity.

Transformation by fire depends, therefore, on our individual choices and capacities to consciously reach both up toward the light of the spirit and down to the emotions and the primordial life of body and earth. Each gesture upward is an invitation to the spirit to flow more abundantly into soul. And each gesture downward an acknowledgment that our healing and wholeness depend on gathering the scattered, dismembered parts of being and offering them as sacrifices on the altar of Self.

From the perspective of Self, the all-consuming fire brings birth and growth. Through its work psychic and physical energies become gradually more in tune with its immortal theme. But from the perspective of the ego personality, that part of us still identified with the personal and ephemeral, the work of the fire is a relentless process of death; a process with which the "outer" circumstances of our lives seem to cooperate. (The word "sacrifice" means to "make holy," which itself is etymologically related to "making whole.")

To resist the dying is to attempt to thwart the necessary and life-bringing process of change. It leads to psychological aridity and stagnation and often to physical disease. But to cooperate with it entails relinquishing all the ego identities and securities, all the physical, material, and psychological props which have buttressed our sense of inner stability, identity, and value. It means allowing the old houses to collapse and the ground to shift, even quake, beneath our feet. Such a radical process of psychological undressing severely challenges our trust in the journey, tempting us into desperate attempts to regain control rather than allow what appears to be the fabric of our life to disintegrate.

For Sally this was the most difficult period of her path. Her terror of the various dimensions of dying turned this time of sacrifice into a prolonged nightmare. The process was heralded, as so often, by a dream. She heard a voice saying that the time had arrived for her to die; that her life so far, devoted as it had been to her own interests, had only been a preparation for this death.

She awoke from the dream sweating and trembling, her heart pounding so fast she found it difficult to breathe. Struggling to gather her conscious faculties, she tried to convince herself that the dream was speaking, as dreams usually did, symbolically; that it was not referring to her need for physical death, but for a psychological dying, a sacrifice of all ego-attachments, all desires, attitudes, and possessions which obstructed her ability to recognize and live the will of Self.

For the rest of the day and for many days and weeks to follow, this psychological interpretation seemed satisfactory. She reflected on those areas of her life which were contaminated by egocentricity and was ashamed to discover how many there were; how many of her actions, feelings, and thoughts still continued to be born from and dictated by her ego personality. As she observed these ego-oriented attitudes, she began to feel she was living a double life. On one level, particularly in meditation, she was aware of the complete fulfillment offered by Self, but at other times she seemed to disregard the existence of this Self and live as though she had forgotten it or had never met it, reaching out to other people or to things for the fulfillment that only the Self can provide.

But while she often forgot the Self, it never seemed to forget her. For whenever she directly or indirectly asked others for what it alone could provide she became aware of a quiet but persistent voice within warning her of the inappropriateness of her action or desire, and simultaneously the outer circumstances seemed to cooperate with this voice by depriving her of the objects of her desire. And all the while her dreams continued to speak of death.

In one of these she dreamed of a woman who could travel freely between Earth and Mars. The woman told Sally that she was next in line for succession to the throne. A male companion of the woman asked her whether she would like to "cross over," meaning to die, for she had work to do on the other side. Unsure whether he meant that if she "crossed over" she would be able, like the woman, to travel in and out of her body, Sally awoke sweating and trembling once again.

And during the waking hours between the dreams, the events of Sally's life appeared to be in league with the messages of death. Relationships, cherished objects and ideas, even her work began to disintegrate and fall away.

One day she was holding an ancient sacred text as she answered the telephone to hear an unknown male voice asking her to collaborate with him on a new interpretation of this classic. Though reluctant to immerse herself again in an area she thought she had left behind, she was also impressed by the coincidence of having the book in her hand as she had answered the telephone. So she agreed at least to meet and discuss the idea.

From that moment the project acquired a life of its own. A publishing contract was signed which seemed to provide her with financial security for the foreseeable future, and she discovered an unexpected reservoir of energy and interest for the work.

At moments in between working she enjoyed the thought that for the first time her interests seemed to be compatible both with financial reward and public recognition, and she felt greatly relieved that the ever-pressing question of how she was to support herself and her daughter seemed to have resolved itself. She allowed fantasies of the book's publication to warm her, enjoying the thought that those who had criticized her for so much, including her move to America, might be persuaded by the size of the project and the ambitious publicity surrounding it to recognize that her values and way of life were not as reprehensible as they had once thought. She fantasized about people writing to her, even coming to visit her, perhaps offering new friendships.

So she was ill prepared for the publisher's rejection of the manuscript when she submitted it two years later; shocked by their comments that it was too obscure and their request that she popularize it. However, eager not to relinquish the professional and financial security virtually guaranteed by the book's publication, she and her collaborator spent another eighteen months trying to satisfy their desires without betraying their sense of truth.

They were useless months. The gap between her views and those of the editors was too large to bridge with cosmetic changes. She questioned her perspective again and again, wondering how she could write what they wanted, but discovered she could not. For even though she was not sure that her own views were the right ones, they were all she had. So she relinquished the project and all the ego-gratifying fantasies connected to it—fantasies she had not known she possessed until this publishing opportunity invited them to consciousness.

She gathered the rejected manuscript into a large brown file and put it on the bottom shelf of a dark cupboard. She did not have to file the fantasies away. They were already dissolving in her shame. Picking up a worn copy of the *Bhagavad Gita* lying beside her bed, she read once more its familiar verses on work:

> Those who lust for earthly power offer sacrifice to the gods of the earth; for soon in this world of men success and power come from work.

> The four orders of men arose from me, in justice to their natures and their works. Know that this work was mine, though I am beyond work in Eternity.

> In the bonds of work I am free, because in them I am free from desires. The man who can see this truth, in his work he finds his freedom.

This was known by men of old times, and thus in their work they found liberation. Do thou therefore thy work in life in the spirit that their work was done.

What is work? What is beyond work? Even some seers see this not aright. I will teach thee the truth of pure work, and this truth shall make thee free.

Know therefore what is work, and also know what is wrong work. And know also of a work that is silence: mysterious is the path of work.

The man who in his work finds silence, and who sees that silence is work, this man in truth sees the Light and in all his works finds peace.

He whose undertakings are free from anxious desire and fanciful thought, whose work is made pure in the fire of wisdom: he is called wise by those who see.

In whatever work he does such a man in truth has peace: he expects nothing, he relies on nothing, and ever has fullness of joy.

He has no vain hopes, he is the master of his soul, he surrenders all he has, only his body works: he is free from sin.

He is glad with whatever God gives him, and he has risen beyond the two contraries here below; he is without jealousy, and in success or in failure he is one: his works bind him not.

He has attained liberation: he is free from all bonds, his mind has found peace in wisdom, and his work is a holy sacrifice. The work of such a man is pure.

Who in all his work sees God, he in truth goes unto God: God is his worship, God is his offering, offered by God in the fire of God.
    (4.12–24; trans. Juan Mascaró, Harmondsworth, England, 1986)

At this point Sally put down the book. She had read enough to allow the dissolution of those parts of her which still hungered for earth recognition and financial security, seeing in them a substitute for that which only Self can ultimately provide. She lay down on her bed enjoying the trickles of serenity and joy moving into the vacuum left by the death of her attachment to outer security and value.

Prior to the birth of Self the duality of work and play tends to define our time. Work, however satisfying and rewarding in its own terms, continues to be motivated, in part, by ego considerations such as financial security, social status, community approval. Only during play, on weekends, on vacation, is there opportunity for actions which express the spontaneity of being rather than the plans and goals of attaining.

And since play has been largely exiled from the material and psychological "necessities" associated with work, it is devalued in comparison, regarded by the Puritan consciousness as little more than fun and relaxation, time to recover from the serious tasks of living rather than an element integral to it. Trapped within this work-play duality, our days acquire a staccato on-off character, rarely permitting all of our being, our creativity, persistence, and responsibility, as well as our joy and inventiveness, to live spontaneously and simultaneously.

With the birth of Self and its integrated perspective, the distinction between work and play dissolves. We recognize that what we do for others we are simultaneously doing for ourselves. The ease and delight of life unveils itself, no longer obscured by the ego goals of prestige or ego fears of financial insecurity which once turned our actions into something to be achieved rather than enjoyed. And the creative, productive nature of life, no longer confined to the place of financial reward, is freed to exist in all actions from washing the dishes to writing a symphony, irrespective of whether they increase our material and social status.

For it is the nature of Self to work, to be creative, and to experience this work simultaneously as play. Not only something to be achieved, but also something joyfully complete at each moment of its happening. It is only ego's ephemeral and limited perspective which distinguishes work from play, productivity from pleasure, by being definitively out of touch with the eternal fulfillment of Self; and by regarding itself as separate and therefore in competition with everyone else for limited resources. This combination of competition, together with the conviction that fulfillment is something other people or things can provide, deprives us of the essential ingredient of play—the sense of creative community with the other, whether this be a person, a thing, or the earth itself.

But the birth of Self only opens the door to the inherent unity of work and play. Before it is possible to live this unity throughout each day, to enjoy each moment as an indivisible blend of creativity, joy, and peace, the ego's illusion of separateness, wherever and in whatever form this still lives, needs to be sacrificed. And this the ego resists.

Fear of poverty and social condemnation persuade us to cling to such goal-oriented fantasies as working for money and prestige rather than for the joy of making a creative contribution. Such is the volume of the fearful voices within us that it can be hard to hear the still voice of Self affirming that work done for others is work done for us; that the well-being of another is the well-being of ourself; and that any material discomfort entailed in this kind of work is insignificant beside the joy it brings.

Obviously, giving priority to considerations of creative service rather than financial security does not mean leading an ascetic or spartan life. For the Self, as we have seen, embraces body as well as spirit. To deny the interests of the body is, therefore, to deny one manifestation of Self. Moreover, relating to and assuming responsibility for the mundane side of life, finding work, a house, and adequate material provisions, is an essential part of the unfolding of our sense of individuality, without which we cannot find Self and relinquish the separateness which was a precondition of its realization. But once this has occurred and we have access to the security which is not dependent on ephemeral things, then Self invites us to surrender all ego-oriented goals so that it may flow in and through us, unobstructed by separatist considerations.

For as Jesus Christ is reported to have said:

No man can serve two masters: for either he will hate the one, and love the other; or else he will hold to the one, and despise the other. Ye cannot serve God and mammon.

Therefore I say unto you, take no thought for your life, what ye shall eat, or what ye shall drink; nor yet for your body, what ye shall put on. Is not the life more than meat, and the body than raiment?

Behold the fowls of the air: for they sow not, neither do they reap, nor gather into barns; yet your heavenly Father feedeth them. Are ye not much better than they?

. . . And why take ye thought for raiment? Consider the lilies of the field, how they grow, they toil not, neither do they spin: And yet I say unto you that even Solomon in all his glory was not arrayed like one of these.

(Matthew 6:24–29)

In providing access to the place of complete fulfillment, the birth of Self enables us to choose our work on the basis of service rather than ego gratification. To discover the extent to which we have shifted from an ego perspective to that of Self it can be useful to ask ourselves such questions as "Would I continue to do the work I do if it brought no financial or social reward?" And "Does my work sufficiently satisfy my needs for creativity and giving?"

The link which ego consciousness has forged between work and material security assumes correctly that physical well-being depends on work; but it also assumes that this work has to have a direct relationship to money or wealth. While we remain bound within the parameters of this ego perspective our material survival appears to depend on our individual endeavor alone. But as consciousness shifts its home from ego to Self, as it relinquishes its identification with the personal and ephemeral, this perspective changes. Just as giving to another and working in the interests of another no longer feel like unselfish acts but instead fundamentally indistinguishable from giving to and working in the interests of one's own humanity, so too is there a parallel shift in the experience and scale of receiving. For just as the human organism is created to feed each cell of the healthy individual body, so too does Self spontaneously feed and take care of each individual being no longer isolated from its abundance by limiting images, ideas, and feelings of separateness and autonomy.

But often at the time when the old ego relationship to work is needing to be sacrificed there is no personal experience of this larger scale of giving and receiving. Some may be blessed with faith, but not many. And yet the sense grows that to continue to work in the old ways would be to betray the nascent Self. We sense an invitation to undertake such a sacrifice so as to free more of our being from the fetters of ego and thereby enable more of Self to flow into the patterns and movements of our days; an invitation to shift the burden of material support, as we shifted the burden of psychological support from our shoulders to those of Self. And we sense that inasmuch as we continue to work, think, and feel from the perspective of ego, we continue to obstruct the Self from enlightening and enlivening our soul and body by filling ourselves with energy frequencies too dull and coarse to resonate with the frequencies of Self.

The transitional period between ego perspective and Self perspective can be particularly hard. For we have to close the door on the old ways and attitudes before we can be nourished by or even glimpse the nature of the new. The only support and guidance we may have at such a moment is a quiet sense that we would like to respond to the invitation from within.

Some of the difficult implications of this transition for Sally came to her through her professional work. Since beginning to work as a psychotherapist she had always charged a set fee, a moderate one designed to provide her with a comfortable but modest standard of living. This had seemed an appropriate way of working, one which recognized and respected her physical and psychological needs and, in so doing, provided her clients with the image of a person in touch with earthly as well as psychological and spiritual needs. If someone could not afford her fee, she would, in certain situations, accept a reduction, but only if this did not seriously threaten the viability of her own way of life. So while her work was largely motivated by her interest in and concern for the nature of human beings, it also operated within the parameters of her material needs.

But one spring embryonic questions about the relationship between money and work coincided with the arrival of a new client, a hard-working single mother of three children who could not afford Sally's regular fee or even her reduced fee. Asking herself whether she wanted to work with this woman for little or no financial gain, Sally experienced the two issues of work and finance spontaneously separating. She recognized that she needed money to live, but also that she did not necessarily need it to come in the form of direct payment for her professional services, though, at that time, she still could not imagine how else it might come. Nevertheless she offered to begin work with the understanding that the woman could choose what she wanted and was able to contribute, and that, even if she chose to give nothing, the work would continue.

For the first year the sessions went well. Sometimes the woman contributed nothing and sometimes she gave a token amount, and this continued to feel all right with Sally. Her other clients were giving regular fees, so she was not facing any financial hardship. Gradually the woman found new confidence by way of the work and soon this was reflected by a promotion at work and a considerable increase in salary. For the first time she had some extra money to spend on herself.

She began appearing for their sessions together in a variety of new clothes. Initially Sally was delighted for her; but as the wardrobe continued to grow she noticed a small but persistent voice inside her resenting that this woman, who was still only paying a token fee for their work together, could afford to buy many more clothes and eat in more expensive restaurants than she herself could. She began to feel used, to find herself irritated at the sight of each new piece of clothing, particularly as her own financial situation had begun to deteriorate around this time due to the coincidence of a number of seemingly unrelated circumstances.

Initially Sally found herself reflecting on the woman's unconscious shadow, the part of her which would keep as much as she could for herself and only give when there was no alternative. She reflected on the psychological deprivation and hunger and the projection of psychological value and fulfillment onto material wealth which often underlie such a relationship to money. But while such considerations assisted Sally's understanding and compassion for the woman, they did little to lessen her resentment. For a while she pondered the idea of suggesting a new financial arrangement to the woman, one which would more accurately reflect her changed financial circumstances. But this fantasy did not bring Sally psychological peace. It felt inappropriate, out of tune with her growing sense that money and work were not necessarily tied together.

One wet afternoon, at the end of a session for which the woman had arrived wearing yet another new skirt, Sally said good-bye and then sat down with her irritation, intent on descending into it, allowing it to lead her to a resolution and healing. She soon noticed that behind the sense of being used was the feeling of being robbed; that it felt as though the woman, in not giving to her, was taking from her, stripping her of the stuff she needed in order to live. She received an image of her skin being ripped from her chest, layer by layer, session by free session. She felt her breath and life forces being sucked from her by this woman who came, took so much, and gave so little. Sally felt drained, with nothing more to give . . . empty.

She lay down, at first too sore, then too depressed to do anything but stare at the wet, grey sky. She could not imagine how she should continue her work. For the old way of exchanging services for money felt inappropriate, dead; and the new way of giving for no reward impossible. How could she give without exhausting her reserves, if she received nothing in return?

And then into her emptiness, silently and gently, flowed the infinite joy and vitality of Self. Immediately the urgency of speaking to the woman about their financial arrangements dissolved, and into its place moved the quiet knowledge that, at the right time, Sally would be able to help her recognize her projections onto money.*

Along with material security, all forms of social support are gradually and sometimes painfully sacrificed in the fire of Self—every way in which we relied on other people, situations, or things for our sense of well-being or security. For the Self can only unfold its being within us with the help of our single-minded attention and loyalty:

> And it came to pass after these things, that God did tempt Abraham, and said unto him, Abraham: and he said, Behold, here I am.

> And he said, Take now thy son, thine only son Isaac, whom thou lovest, and get thee into the land of Moriah; and offer him there for a burnt offering upon one of the mountains which I will tell thee of.

> And Abraham rose up early in the morning, and saddled his ass, and took two of his young men with him, and Isaac his son, and clave the wood for the burnt offering, and rose up, and went unto the place of which God had told him. . . . And Abraham took the wood of the burnt offering, and laid it upon Isaac his son; and he took the fire in his hand, and a knife; and they went both of them together.

> And Isaac spake unto Abraham his father, and said, My father: and he said, Here am I, my son. And he said, Behold the fire and the wood: but where is the lamb for a burnt offering?

> And Abraham said, My son, God will provide himself a lamb for a burnt offering: so they went both of them together.

---

*Charging a standard fee has, of course, significant psychological implications for the client as well as the therapist, apart from the ones discussed earlier. For money is a potent symbol of value, and therefore paying a fee can help the patient to value the work. Moreover, having to pay for therapy can assist those who have difficulty accepting the practical realities and limitations of earthly existence in taking responsibility for the ordinary, material aspects of life. However, in a good therapeutic relationship these issues will arise anyway regardless of financial arrangements.

And they came to the place which God had told him of; and Abraham built an altar there, and laid the wood in order, and bound Isaac his son, and laid him on the altar upon the wood.

And Abraham stretched forth his hand, and took the knife to slay his son.

And the angel of the Lord called unto him out of heaven, and he said, Here am I.

And he said, Lay not thine hand upon the lad, neither do thou any thing unto him: for now I know that thou fearest God, seeing thou has not withheld thy son, thine only son from me.

And Abraham lifted up his eyes, and looked, and beheld behind him a ram caught in a thicket by his horns: and Abraham went and took the ram and offered him up for a burnt offering in the stead of his son.

(Genesis 22:1–13)

The act of sacrifice, which forms a fundamental part of all religious and esoteric teaching, involves the death or surrender of an ephemeral mode of being, a transitory or personal manifestation of cosmic energy, in the interests of the eternal and transcendent. As Abraham's story reflects, God, as the divinity or Self indwelling each person, is intent not on depriving us of those we love but only on severing our attachment to these people so the psychic energy locked in these dependent relationships might be released for the further unfolding of the unconditional love of Self, the love which asks and wants nothing but the well-being and fulfillment of the other, his or her union with the source of eternal life.

And behold, one came and said unto him, Good Master, what good thing shall I do, that I may have eternal life? And he said unto him, Why callest thou me good? there is none good but one, that is God: but if thou wilt enter into life, keep the commandments. . . .

The young man saith unto him, All these things have I kept from my youth up: what lack I yet?

Jesus said unto him, If thou wilt be perfect, go and sell that thou hast, and give to the poor, and thou shalt have treasure in heaven: and come and follow me.

But when the young man heard that saying, he went away sorrowful: for he had great possessions.

Then said Jesus unto his disciples, Verily I say unto you, That a rich man shall hardly enter into the kingdom of heaven.

And again I say unto you, It is easier for a camel to go through the eye of a needle, than for a rich man to enter into the kingdom of God.

When his disciples heard it, they were exceedingly amazed, saying, Who then can be saved?

But Jesus beheld them and said unto them, With men this is impossible; but with God all things are possible.

Then answered Peter and said unto him, Behold, we have forsaken all, and followed thee; what shall we have therefore?

And Jesus said unto them, Verily I say unto you, That ye which have followed me, in the regeneration when the Son of man shall sit in the throne of his glory, ye also shall sit upon twelve thrones, judging the twelve tribes of Israel. And every one that hath forsaken houses, or brethren, or sister, or father, or mother, or wife, or children, or lands, for my name's sake, shall receive a hundredfold, and shall inherit everlasting life.

But many that are first shall be last; and the last shall be first.

(Matthew 19:16–30)

Whether we disposess ourselves physically and socially, whether we give all our belongings to the poor and become a hermit, is less relevant than psychological dispossession. Which, of course, is not to say that such tangible and visible dispossessions might not be of psychological assistance to some people at certain moments on their journey. But the significant task is to dispossess ourselves so completely that it is psychologically irrelevant whether we are living in a hut with one bowl and a thin mat or in a mansion with three cars, a swimming pool, a husband, four children, a dog, and a goldfish. For regardless of our earthly circumstances, our only attachment at this moment of our becoming is to Self as it lives as each of us and as the earth herself.

Since looking to others for the fulfillment of our own psychological hungers means turning away from the source of all fulfillment, the Self asks if we are willing to subordinate all desires to the desire for it; to become single-minded expressions of it. For being universal and eternal, Self can only unite with a soul which has realized universality, which has become an empty vessel, released from the clutter of personal and ephemeral attachments.

Just as prior to the realization of Self, it is necessary for consciousness to descend into the depths of the unconscious—to find, suffer, enjoy, and integrate aspects of soul hitherto identified with body, matter, and emotion, to withdraw its positive and negative projections onto others and things—so after the birth of Self it is necessary not only to continue this work, but also to nourish the infant Self by tuning into its being through regular meditation as well as during other moments in the day.

Doing this requires a different orientation to our psychological work. Following each new integration of energy, each withdrawal of projection, we need to move beyond the personal relationship to this energy, and instead of holding on to the feelings of individual expansion and enrichment it has brought, we need to offer these up to the sacrificial flames of Self. For example, an attractive man might awaken a woman's hitherto unconscious desires for a particular type of masculine beauty. She might easily fall in love with him, even after the birth of Self. But now she needs not only to withdraw the projection in the same way that she has withdrawn previous projections—by amplifying the image of his beauty and absorbing it into her soul until it finds its life and reality as an integral part of her, independent of the outer man—she needs also to surrender any sense of private or personal possession of this energy by giving it to Self. For the process of individual expansion which awakens us to Self needs, at this stage, to reach out and embrace the cosmos without losing touch with its own unique path on this earth. Within the body this process is experienced as a shift of focus from the heart to the crown chakra, from feeling Self as an individual spark of the divine to uniting with the source of the light itself.

The two processes of becoming—the one which precedes and the one which succeeds the birth of Self—occur by way of two different levels of sacrifice. To find soul and its source, the Self, it is necessary to sacrifice identification with body and matter, to differentiate physical and psychic energy, reclaiming those parts of us which we hitherto met by way of "outer" objects and people, so that soul may unfold and matter reveal itself as merely one level of our manifestation. After the birth of Self it is necessary to sacrifice all personal identification with the newly differentiated and integrated feeling and thought energy, that it may reunite with and nourish the unfolding Self.

Such a sacrifice of personal needs and desires is, of course, only appropriate after we have completed enough of our healing journey into emotion, body, and instinct, recognized our hungers and connected with the source of infinite abundance—the Self. Prior to this, any sacrifice of need can only occur by way of denial and dissociation. At the expense, in other words, of our total well-being and becoming, and therefore of our capacity for recognizing, nourishing, and loving the becoming of others.

After the unfolding of Self, after we have glimpsed and even ventured a toe into the promised land, we are unlikely to be able to remain there for any consistent length of time, more often backsliding for hours, days, even weeks, as we forget the warmth and joy of the human Eden and are overwhelmed by the desolation which characterizes the passage between the ego-oriented perspective and the one of Self.

Sally had many opportunities to suffer the coldness of this passage after her arrival in America. But one occasion in particular helped her to understand the nature of the sacrifice which was required if she was to reconnect with the joy and abundance of Self.

It was over a year since she and Rachael had left England. Rachael had found a few friends at her new school, but Sally had found none. She had met some people she liked, but their lives were already too full of work, family, and old friends to have time for more than occasional meetings with her. She felt very alone. Increasingly she noticed herself looking forward to 4:00 p.m., when Rachael returned from school, not only to find out how her day had gone but also for the pleasure of being with someone. The next few hours were usually full of talk, cooking, eating, and reading stories—warm, nourishing hours. But then after 8:00 p.m., when Rachael went to bed, the house was quiet again. Sally would gravitate toward her down duvet with a hot water bottle and reflect on her work or read. But, after a day of doing similar things, neither of these activities were usually sufficiently interesting to protect her from the loneliness which haunted these evenings. Like a damp cloud it seemed to creep under the duvet with her, sucking cold hollows out of her heart. In the beginning it did not stay long, but as the months passed its icy presence strengthened. She found herself fantasizing about the home she had left, about people she loved, friends, even distant acquaintances whom she had once ignored but would now be delighted to see.

Sometimes the cold became so acute that even the duvet and hot water bottle seemed frozen by its presence. So the telephone call from Caroline, the only person she had met since her arrival with whom she felt the seeds of a possible friendship, delighted and also surprised her. For she had made a number of overtures to her after their first meeting, all of which collapsed through Caroline's apparent lack of interest. But this evening Caroline was talking freely about the difficulties she was having with her work and her husband, and even suggested they meet for a more extended conversation. They fixed a time, and Sally hung up the receiver, poignantly aware of how one relatively short telephone call could fill her with so much warmth.

Two days later Caroline arrived. Sally's pleasure in seeing her at least equaled if not surpassed her fantasies. For a while Caroline went on talking, as she had on the telephone, about her work and her marital problems. Sally listened, delighting in the presence of another adult in her sitting room. And then she began to talk—telling Caroline a little of the loneliness of moving to a new country, of looking after Rachael without the practical or psychological support of friends and relatives. Caroline's sympathy helped to dissolve some of the pain. Sally breathed in the warmth and began to relax deeper into her chair, inwardly smiling at the death of loneliness this burgeoning friendship would bring.

"One of the reasons I suggested we meet today," said Caroline, "was to ask if you would be my therapist." Her words stifled Sally's smile. At another time she knew she would have been delighted to have a new client, particularly one with whom she felt such rapport. But now she could only feel the skin-ripping pain of this embryonic friendship being torn away.

Fortunately, their conversation was interrupted at this moment by Rachael's return from school. So while Caroline and Rachael talked, Sally had time to listen to her pain; to feel the part of her which longed to say "No" to Caroline's request, longed to tell her that what she wanted was a friend, not a new client. But beneath the pain, she also heard the familiar quiet voice of Self suggesting she consent. So she told Caroline she would like to think about it for a few days.

But she didn't need more than one day. For Sally awoke the next morning with her loneliness dissolved by the warm, fulfilling presence of Self. She called Caroline to say "Yes."

For the waters of Self to flow freely, for our souls to be continually bathed in their strength, wisdom, and love, our consciousness needs to be empty, still, and receptive. In reaching out for emotional support after the birth of Self, we turn away from its infinite warmth

and support, filling our being with emotions, pleasurable and painful, whose very existence obstructs the flowing presence of Self.

Caroline's request at that moment in Sally's life provided her with
an opportunity to recognize the degree to which her desire for
friendship had been a desire for support, a desire to receive from
outside the warmth accessible within. And to recognize that inasmuch as it was born from this emotional hunger, it conflicted with
her relationship to Self and therefore with her capacity to give to
Caroline.

With precision timing, the pattern of our lives seems to assist our
sacrifice of all that obstructs a freely flowing connection to Self, by
depriving us of the objects of our desires—friends, lovers, professional security, ideological systems, money—even the teachers or
therapists whose wisdom and love have enabled us to travel this far.

Soon after Sally had begun working with Caroline she dreamed
that she was about to take the final examinations which would certify
her as a Jungian analyst. Nine months later she dreamed that she
had just passed these examinations and was in Zurich to receive her
diploma from the International Association of Jungian Psychology.

The time between these two dreams coincided with a gradual loss
of interest in studying other people's psychological theories and
conceptual systems, even those authors for whom Sally had profound
respect and to whom she felt psychologically indebted. It was not
so much that she questioned these people's perceptions, though this
occurred, but more that each time she studied other people's insights
she felt she was taking a circuitous route to truth when a more direct
one was available to her.

So she began to devote herself singlemindedly to this direct way,
allowing her inner experience of spirit, soul and earth to be her only
book, studying it as it revealed itself to her in each moment: as the
dappled sunlight through autumn leaves, a dream, the angry remark
of a bus driver, or the stone reliefs of Christ accompanied by the
sacred beasts on the portal of the cathedral at Chartres. Happily she
put away the books which no longer interested her, relinquishing
the conceptual baggage she had borrowed from others, the lenses
through which she had created and understood her reality, and
welcomed the multitude of questions which took their place.

Integral to this process was the feeling that the time had come to
stop seeing her analyst, not because she considered her own therapy
complete but because she felt sufficiently in touch with her inner

therapist to continue the journey into darkness unaccompanied by an outer one.

When she began to speak of these things to her therapist, he questioned her with his customary perception and understanding. But during their final hour together his attitude changed. He coldly suggested that she was not only leaving him but also depth psychology and soul work.

Until this moment she had always felt his support for her own path, wherever this had led her. But now he seemed to be opposing it, trying to undermine her confidence in her capacity to recognize and follow the river of her own becoming. Tears came to her eyes. The decision to leave the familiar and collectively approved way of working already felt lonely, and now even her own therapist was doubting her motivations.

For a while she allowed the doubts to eat into her, to erode the core of warmth which had supported her through other solitary steps and to undermine the quiet confidence born from the dreams. She realized how much she had relied on him for his approval and support. Her work with him and her two previous analysts had helped her to hear, respect, and act on her inner directions. In the course of doing so she had become used to her soul journey being questioned, doubted, and often criticized by friends and acquaintances, even by those closest to her. But not by her analyst. This opened a new dimension of aloneness.

She sat for a while, silent as the tears dripped down her cheeks. She waited, not knowing what to do or say. And then, amid the painful feeling of betrayal, she found the confidence to walk her way, irrespective of his approval or anyone else's. She got up, shook his hand, and said, "Thank you."

Then she left, not realizing until she was driving home through the late afternoon traffic that what she had really thanked him for was not their work together but his final doubts. For in withdrawing his confidence in her he had enabled her to find her own, a confidence that no one could take away.

Unwittingly he had created for her a valuable rite of passage.

Our advanced industrial world is largely devoid of rites of passage. Other religious traditions, like that of the American Indians, are perhaps more fortunate:

I had come to Eagle Man that morning in some excitement, to report on the last mission, during which interesting things had happened which he would like to hear . . . .

He did not smile. He did not look at me. His face was drawn and grim, the face of a hostile stranger. His voice when he spoke was harsh and loud.

"You won't like what I say. I'm going to stamp on your toes. Give me your Pipe. You been misusing it."

If he had run me through with a spear I couldn't have been more shocked. A sharp pain went through my solar plexus. I wasn't armored against a psychic wound, in this place, from this man. I had never imagined needing protection from Eagle Man. I stared at him dazed.

He shouted, "Give me your Pipe."

I said, "Why?"

He said, "Never mind why! You have been using it wrong. You have been showing off."

Then anger came and outrage. I forgot that one must not interrupt nor contradict a Medicine Man. I found some sort of voice to protest, "That isn't true!"

"Don't argue," he said, "just give me your Pipe." . . .

He stepped toward me, strong and menacing. All certainties, all comforts were gone from this familiar place. It was a chasm of violence and terror, into which I would fall, when I had finished bleeding. . . . I didn't remember to call to the Grandfathers for help. I couldn't think of anything, but from somewhere far away, a spark of strength stood up in me to say:

"No. I won't give you my Pipe . . . . I can't give you my Pipe. It isn't mine to give. It belongs to the Great Spirit."

His face changed. Something came back from wherever it had gone. His eyes were almost the eyes I knew. I spoke to them, with tremulous breath. . . .

"You made my Pipe and I shall always be thankful, but you didn't give it to me. Power Man gave it to me. He blessed it in his Sweat."

This seemed to enrage him again.

"I don't care what Power Man did! Give me your Pipe!"

"I can't," I pleaded, as if he must understand, "it isn't mine to give." . . .

I willed myself to look at him, and so we stood, facing each other questioningly. There was a change in the room now. I saw that he believed me. He said, more gently:

"Go and get the Pipe."

I took the Pipe out of its Bag and presented it to him in a sacred manner.

He took it from me ritually. He wiped it over with a long piece of sage that he had ready on a table beside him. Then he smudged it with burning sweet grass. He handed it back to me, and motioned toward the Bag. He smudged that too, took the Pipe and put it in, tying up the ends in the special symmetrical way I could never master.

Then he straightened himself and smiled.

"Well," he said, "you done your part."

But sadness came with understanding. When he smudged the Pipe, he had cut the ties between us. Something was gone that could not be restored. My Pipe was no longer "under Eagle Man's Pipe." This was Graduation, a long-worked-for achievement, but a rough and lonely one.

(Evelyn Eaton, *I Send a Voice,* Wheaton, Ill., 1978, pp. 172–75)

In itself sacrifice is insufficient preparation for union with Self. It needs to be accompanied by the conscious choice not merely to cooperate with and suffer the losses, the old props and securities, but also to relinquish the desires themselves; to consciously shed the emotional way of relating to the world; and stand resolutely within the psychological emptiness which results.

For each of us there is likely to be one attachment, one desire, beside whose sacrifice the rest feel somewhat insignificant. For Abraham it was his son Isaac. For Sally it was her physical life.

The dreams foretelling her death continued to arrive. And with each one Sally found it harder to rest with the fantasy that all they referred to was a psychological death. She became obsessively sensitive to each twinge or ache in her body. Her heart rate, already rapid as a result of the recent years of almost incessant stress, was now rarely under 100 beats per minute, and usually higher.

The nights were particularly stressful. For she knew her body needed sleep if it was to withstand the impact of such chronic high anxiety; and because she knew this, she naturally could not sleep, but struggled through the long night hours worrying about the inaccessible sleep she was too tense to receive. The worst time was between one and four in the morning. Then the house was quiet, Rachael and, as she imagined, everyone else asleep, while she sweated with fear about the death which every anxious moment only seemed to bring closer.

As the insomnia increased she turned to sleeping tablets. At first these proved quite successful. She managed to get some drugged sleep, and though disliking their toxic residues which she could feel swimming around her body for much of the following day, it was a considerable relief to have a modicum of energy with which to perform essential tasks. But they soon lost their power to defeat her terror. When this happened she would lie in bed, heavily drugged, but definitely awake, suffering a new dimension of terror as she reflected that there was no recourse now, nothing to save her from death by exhaustion. After nights like these, she would get up in the morning to another terrifying day—hours of trying to cope with looking after the house and Rachael while her body and soul screamed for the rest her terror deprived her.

Though she realized with wry humor that she was more likely to die of fear than any disease or stroke of fate, she could not see what she could do about it except to continue to struggle and fight; to hold onto life with every ounce of determination she had. For the fear, born from her attachment to life, had gripped her soul.

Sometimes she used the sleepless hours to reflect on the psychology of her terror, to imaginatively experience the different deaths which seemed to fill her fantasies. The fear of death had been with her as long as she could remember. As a young girl she had been haunted by the image of being buried alive—suffocating in a closed coffin six feet underground. She had spent many hours imagining how she could leave instructions to her relatives to check and double check that she was completely dead before she was buried. But as she recalled that image now she realized it had lost its potency. Her fear of death no longer seemed to be connected with the mode of death, the process of dying, nor with the state of being dead. Rather it seemed to revolve exclusively around the fear of giving up life. She did not want to stop living. This realization surprised her considerably. For her life had not been easy; indeed, it had been a catalog of difficulties and pain. So why, she wondered, did she so much want it to continue that the want itself was in danger of killing her? One immediate answer was Rachael. The thought of the pain her death would cause her was possibly the worst fantasy. The image of Rachael's devastated face at the news of her death was sufficient to spur Sally into another round of fighting. But besides this she also realized her own deep interest and attachment to earth life, to its opportunities for loving and learning.

After six months of almost constant fear and sleeplessness her body was so weak that she barely had the strength to wash or cook the simplest meal for herself and Rachael. Driving had become too

risky as the weakness caused unpredictable periods of extreme faint-
ness, moments during which she would suddenly be too weak even
to lift her arm.

One evening, in desperation, she took four sleeping pills, thinking
that for one night at least she would get some sleep. But they had
no effect at all apart from making her feel sick and drugged. Wide
awake, she sweated out the hours, alternately trying to relax, to see
more clearly the object of her fear and to answer the endless question
of why this was happening to her.

Finally, around dawn, she fell asleep. A few moments later she
found herself floating above the bed, then moving around the room
trying to turn on the lights. But none of the light switches responded
to her touch. Puzzled, she guessed that there must have been a
power outage. With this thought she felt a jolt, a kind of rapid
snapping sensation, and found herself lying in bed with her hands
reaching for the bedside light switch. But this time the light worked.
She smiled ruefully to herself. For she had always been interested in
out-of-body experiences, fascinated by other people's descriptions
of them, so she found it ironic that her first one should be entirely
preoccupied with turning on the lights, dispelling the darkness which
shrouded her fear of death.

She was also interested to realize that while floating around her
bedroom she had been able to see almost as well as if she had been
in her body. The only thing she could not do was to operate at the
physical level. She could see the light switch, but she could not turn
it on.

Remembering this enabled her to imagine a little of the immediate
post-death state and to understand the numerous accounts of people
who during their near-death experiences were bewildered by the
fact that they could see their relatives and friends, hear their weeping,
and yet be unable to physically communicate with them.

But this first astral experience did more than convince Sally of the
reality of life after death. It also convinced her that there was no
outer solution to her terror. With this conviction, she got up, washed
briefly, and poured the remainder of the sleeping pills down the
toilet. Then she made herself some warm milk and honey and got
back into bed. Propped up on pillows, she waited for Rachael to
come in for a morning hug on her way to school.

After Rachael had left, Sally continued to lie in bed as she always
did these days, too weak to do anything else. But this morning,

though physically exhausted, she felt psychologically strong. For now she had decided to take death on single-handed, without the assistance of toxic drugs or anything else.

The day passed quite calmly. Night came and Sally turned off the lights and waited, hoping that without the support of sleeping pills, her body would eventually sleep through sheer exhaustion. But such a hope did not account for the real strength of her terror, much stronger it seemed than her body's need for sleep. So the first night passed with no sleep at all, not even a brief five or ten minutes. The second and third nights passed in the same way. By the fourth day Sally was so weak she could barely speak.

That night was the turning point. For by the fifth morning, still not having slept, the mental and physical agony had broken her will to fight death. Instead of trying to resist it, to take it on in battle, to flee from it as she had done now for over a year, she gave up the battle. "All right, Lord or whoever, whatever you are," she said, "all right, author of my dreams, I will die if that is what you want. I am tired of this fight."

For the first time Sally turned her face toward death and accepted it. She lay in her bed, allowing the most terrifying and painful images to come before her eyes, and accepted each one of them. She imagined never seeing the earth again, the beauty of its spring. She even imagined Rachael returning from school to find her dead. She felt the sadness. And she said good-bye. Good-bye to each attachment she had to living on this earth, to every personal reason for continuing to be here.

When she had finished her good-byes, had allowed all the sadness to flow through her, she lay still and waited for death. Perhaps for the first time in her life she completely relaxed. And then she fell asleep.

Over the next days and weeks a rhythm of sleep returned to her. Occasionally she touched the old fear. But when she felt its icy presence she was able to recognize it as evidence of attachment and relinquish it in exchange for peace. One morning she awoke feeling that for the first time the nightmare had truly passed. That night, in a dream, the quiet and by now familiar all-knowing voice spoke to her:

"Your trials have only just begun. Your future is a life of sacrifice: the sacrifice of everything you own, everything you have, and everything you desire."

The Self acts like the vortex of a whirlpool. Once born into consciousness, it slowly but relentlessly sucks all of our energies from their scattered places at the periphery of being back into our center and source, into itself. We can cooperate with this process of ego-death and Self-becoming, or we can fight it. Either way, our attachments and personal identifications will finally be destroyed, dissolved by the greater power of the soul intent on remembering and uniting with Self.

We descended lower, and I watched in awe as pieces of foam flew up into the air, and logs drifting on the river's edge were caught in the force of the whirlpool, pulled under, and disappeared.

"That is where we come from," Zoila said in my ear. She pointed at the middle of the whirlpool with her stick. "It is to that mystery we are trying to return."

My eyes could bear only so much of looking into the whirlpool. I leaned a little against Zoila for support, feeling clumsy and ungainly. She moved with such grace. We were both dripping wet from the heat and the gathering moisture of mist and spray. I noticed big liquid drops running down the sides of Zoila's face.

She turned to me and said, "See the vanishing point in the center. That is the void. Watch how a path is created by ripples spiraling out from the center. You were born of the void, and the swell is like the outwardness of things. This is like our earth walk. In our youth and ignorance we walk farther and farther from the center, until we are very far away from our original nature. That is how life is. That is its pattern. Most of us live way out on the perimeter of the spiral. Then, at some point in life, something special happens to you—an insight, a death—and you begin to wonder about yourself and ask questions. 'What does life mean? Where do I come from?' Has this not happened to you?"

"Yes."

"Haven't you wondered why it is difficult to find your true nature?"

"Yes, I have tried to find my way home."

"Go back to the source. Watch the whirlpool. From such powers the universe has evolved. The powers of the universe are within you. See how everything is swallowed into the center. It is ordained that all be pulled in. The universe will feed into itself, and all creatures great and small will be liberated."

(Lynn V. Andrews, *Jaguar Woman: And the Wisdom of the Butterfly Tree*, San Francisco, 1985, pp. 87–88)

Many years before the publication of *Jaguar Woman*, Sally had dreamed her own version of Zoila's wisdom: *She found herself* traveling on foot along a spiraling road which led to the center of the vortex, the crater of the volcano. When she reached this center, she merged with its heat and light, becoming one with the source of warmth and life itself. Reborn as this center, she noticed that she was now a radiant androgynous being returning to the world on the back of an ass.

Chapter Seven

A LONGER LIFE

As we relinquish our attachment to and identification with people, objects, social contexts, even life itself, and the energy previously locked in these dependencies is sacrificed in the fires of Self, our consciousness is released from outworn and inappropriate definitions of itself:

A daughter came to the preaching cloister and asked for Meister Eckhart. The doorman asked:
"Whom shall I announce?"
"I don't know," she said.
"Why don't you know?"
"Because I am neither a girl, nor a woman, nor a husband, nor a wife, nor a widow, nor a virgin, nor a master, nor a maid, nor a servant."
The doorman went to Meister Eckhart and said:
"Come out here and see the strangest creature you ever heard of. Let me go with you, and you stick your head out and ask 'Who wants me?'"
Meister Eckhart did so and she gave him the same reply she had made to the doorman. Then he said:
"My dear child, what you say is right and sensible but explain to me what you mean." She said:
"If I were a girl, I should be still in my first innocence; if I were a woman, I should always be giving birth in my soul to the eternal word;

if I were a husband, I should put up a stiff resistance to all evil; if I were a wife, I should keep faith with my dear one, whom I married; if I were a widow, I should always be longing for the one I loved; if I were a virgin, I should be reverently devout; if I were a servant-maid, in humility I should count myself lower than God or any creature; and if I were a manservant, I should be hard at work, always serving my Lord with my whole heart. But since of all these, I am neither one, I am just a something among somethings, and so I go."

Then Meister Eckhart went in and said to his pupils: "It seems to me that I have just listened to the purest person I have ever known."

(Meister Eckhart, trans. Raymond B. Blackney, New York, pp. 252–53)

The sacrifice of all identification with social role, sex, or anything else other than the universal and eternal Self contributes to and fosters our capacity for relationship. It enables appreciation in place of obsession, love in place of desire, perception and understanding in place of projection, and thereby enhances rather than inhibits our ability to perform the functions of husband, wife, banker, or poet. For instead of feeling "I am a poet," "I am a banker," or "I am a psychotherapist," we regard ourselves, like Meister Eckhart's daughter, to be something among somethings, people who have chosen to take on a particular work and role and are glad to perform it with quiet persistence, joy, and responsibility for as long as it feels necessary and useful. But when circumstances change and such a role ceases to be available or appropriate we have no difficulty in relinquishing it, for none of our well-being or identity is dependent on it.

Such independence of soul from its different physical forms and various personalities not only enables a more compassionate and wiser connection to body and earth in that we are able to see and appreciate them for what they are, rather than for how they may provide for our fulfillment; it also offers access to dimensions of being reachable beyond the limits of birth and death.

Following a heart attack which brought him close to death, Jung had a vision in which he was approaching a temple:

I had the feeling that everything was being sloughed away; everything I aimed at or wished for or thought, the whole phantasmagoria of earthly existence, fell away or was stripped from me—an extremely painful process. Nevertheless something remained; it was as if I now carried along with me everything I had ever experienced or done, everything that had happened around me. I might also say: it was with me, and I was it. I consisted of all that, so to speak. I consisted of my own history, and I felt with great certainty: this is what I am. "I am this bundle of what has been, what has been accomplished."

This experience gave me a feeling of extreme poverty, but at the same time of great fullness. There was no longer anything I wanted or desired. I existed in an objective form; I was what I had been and lived. At first the sense of annihilation predominated, of having been stripped or pillaged; but suddenly that became of no consequence. Everything seemed to be past; what remained was a *fait accompli*, without any reference back to what had been. There was no longer any regret that something had dropped away or been taken away. On the contrary: I had everything that I was, and that was everything.

Something else engaged my attention: as I approached the temple I had the certainty that I was about to enter an illuminated room and would meet there all those people to whom I belong in reality. There I would at last understand—this too was a certainty—what historical nexus I or my life fitted into. I would know what had been before me, why I had come into being, and where my life was flowing. My life as I lived it had often seemed to me like a story that has no beginning and no end. I had the feeling that I was a historical fragment, an excerpt for which the preceding and succeeding text was missing. My life seemed to have been snipped out of a long chain of events, and many questions had remained unanswered.

(*Memories, Dreams, Reflections*, pp. 290–91)

According to Jung's autobiography his vision stopped at this point, for he found himself called back to his body.* But many others have remembered some of the larger context which gives meaning to the fragments of a single life. For Sally the images began to surface by way of a series of dreams about dynastic Egypt. But it was a Hollywood television film about Tutankhamen which constellated the most shocking and painful memory.

She was sitting in her favorite position, legs tucked under her, on the large, soft sofa. Her American friend Chris was in the armchair. They had just enjoyed a good dinner and were both feeling a quiet

*Whether or not Jung believed in reincarnation remains unclear. According to Jungian therapist Evlo van Waveren, Jung did believe in it. "I once spoke to Professor Jung about this subject and later his wife came to me and said 'Don't talk to anyone about this, the time isn't right for it.' So I kept quiet, because the world to which Professor Jung wanted to prove that there *was* such a thing as the psyche wouldn't have gone along with the notion of reincarnation." (Jonathan Cott, *The Search for Omm Sety*, New York, 1987, p. 202.)

pleasure in being together. The film was not particularly well made, but it contained some good shots of the Valley of the Kings, which had fascinated Sally since she had begun to dream of ancient Egypt.

In the middle of one of these scenes she turned to Chris to see if he was sharing her interest, only to be profoundly shocked by the appearance of his face. His normally strong and kind features were now twisted by cruelty. Repulsed and frightened, Sally turned back to the film. But she was unable to concentrate. Chris's face was a far more compelling image than Hollywood Egypt. Cautiously she looked at him again, hoping that the cruel expression would have vanished. But it had intensified, changing his features so radically that it was almost impossible to recognize him.

Shocked into silence and immobility, Sally continued to stare at him. And as she did so images began to form spontaneously in the space between them, a second movie, surpassing the TV one in intensity and realism. A movie in which she and Chris were the principal actors.

She saw and felt herself as the mummified body of an Egyptian woman, lying in a coffin in a dark tomb. The coffin lid was off, and Sally had the strange sensation of experiencing herself simultaneously in and out of her body. She felt entombed and mummified, while simultaneously hovering about six feet above the coffin, looking down at her body.

Suddenly, as she watched, a man, the same man, it seemed, though in a different body than the one now sitting opposite her in the armchair, forced his way into the tomb and, pulling out a dagger, stabbed her repeatedly in the throat. Continuing to identify with both the prostrate woman and the hovering soul, Sally experienced the slow pain of dying as well as the untroubled, though interested perspective of the observer.

As the images of murder faded, she sat, unable to move or speak. The shock and remembered pain of the stab wounds seemed to consume her.

Enough of what she was going through must have registered on her face, for Chris left his armchair and moved toward her, asking her gently what was wrong. He was, of course, somewhat perplexed by the violence with which she recoiled from his presence. And since she was still dumb from shock, there was little she could do to explain the situation.

Gradually, however, the power of the images diminished. Chris's face resumed its familiar appearance, and Sally's fear subsided sufficiently for her to be able to speak.

Since the beginning of their relationship Sally had occasionally noticed in herself a seemingly irrational fear of Chris arising in response to certain of his gestures or actions, a fear which often provoked reactions in her which were out of proportion to the incident. Initially she worked with these fearful fantasies as projections of her own unconscious cruelty. But even after considerable work admitting her own ugliness into consciousness, some of the fear persisted. So while the horrifying vision of having been murdered by him in another life left many questions unresolved—such as the motivation for the murder and why she simultaneously experienced the incident from an in-body and an out-of-body perspective—it nevertheless enabled her to understand these episodes of fear and to discriminate better between what belonged to their relationship in this life and what was a remnant from their unhappy past.

But the value to her of remembering this past life was not restricted to her relationship with Chris. The incident in front of the television was followed by a dream sequence reflecting aspects of this former life and reconnecting her with forgotten psychological and spiritual wealth.

In the first dream she was standing in an Egyptian valley holding a delicate crystal vase and facing a soaring sandstone rock on whose summit stood the pantheon of Egyptian gods and goddesses, including some of the kings. Although she could see that the figures were made of stone, she also knew that they were alive.

Her attention was particularly drawn to the figures of Rameses II, a monkey god, and a cow's tail. As she gazed at them, stirred by their power and familiarity, a voice told her to choose the god or goddess with whom she felt the greatest affinity. Without understanding why, but moved by their capacity to communicate telepathically, she chose a pair of "living" statues called the "miraculous twins."

Having chosen, she was invited to begin her ascent to the divinities, climbing a narrow, precipitous trail which twisted its way up the high sandstone rockface. Two friends accompanied her: a man who had supported her through many lonely and difficult periods of her life and her ex-sister-in-law. They climbed single file, the only way possible on the narrow trail. Sally walked cautiously, gripping the knee-high glass handrail, which was all that existed between her and the sheer drop to the valley floor on her left.

After ascending in this way for a considerable time she reached a flat rock, where she was told she had to change her clothes and say good-bye to her companions. Taking off her twentieth-century skirt and shirt, she put on the pale yellowy-cream robe of an Egyptian priestess which had been laid out for her. As she ritually undressed, stripping both body and soul of its unnecessary clothing, a woman came up the path behind her, riding a horse and leading a group of people. Sally was astonished at the confidence and ease with which this woman climbed the trail, until she realized that the woman had traveled this way many times before. She was also surprised to notice that when the woman and her group reached the clothes-changing place, they discarded riding clothes for conventional Western style suits and continued up the trail leading toward a monastery. As they climbed, Sally overheard the woman telling her group that some of the houses in the village of the gods were inhabited by evil spirits but that there was no cause for concern since the monastery had a delightful atmosphere. Sally noted the warning, for the village of the gods, not the monastery, was her destination.

Among other things, the dream indicated that Sally could only reach the village of the gods, and in particular the "miraculous twins," if she was willing to divest herself of every vestige of the personal and particular, everything related to her personality, her age, her cultural and educational background; if she was willing, in other words, to become the priestess, one whose soul is sufficiently free of the clutter of personal attachments and relationships that it is able to mediate between heaven and earth. The dream also made it clear that the starting point of such a divestment and journey toward the spirit is on the valley floor, holding the crystal vase. For until we have entered into the valley of our being, made contact with the deep ravines of body and instinct and found our crystal vase—the pure receptivity of soul which alone can contain and reflect the flowers of Self—we are not ready to begin the ascent to the transpersonal realms. But once we have discovered our individual relationship to Self, connected with the psychological strength and purity which enable us to hold the tension of the opposites sufficiently for Self to unfold, it is necessary to relinquish all personal relationships to Self for one which replaces the duality of I and Thou, crystal vase and nectar of life, with a transcendent union; an indivisibility of God and soul, a communion with the village of the gods.

There is a tendency among some depth psychologists to focus, in their dream interpretations, on the similarities between different cultures; to regard, for example, the great mother goddesses of ancient

Greece, Rome, India, and Egypt as archetypal images of a similar level of archetypal energy. Although this horizontal perspective can provide insight into the many faces of a single archetype, thereby facilitating the recognition of its energy, it is unable to distinguish between the different levels of consciousness at which the great mother goddess can live and be experienced. These levels traverse the entire gamut of creation, from body to spirit, enabling the mother goddess to be seen in a mother's physical nourishing of her children, in the warm, nutritious breast milk, as well as at every other level of being—from the raw, vital, and instinctual energy of the primitive earth mother to the refined delicacy and translucent spirituality of the Virgin Mary.

From this vertical perspective the images of ancient Egypt are psychologically distinct from those of ancient Greece or India. A dream about ancient Egyptian religious practices introduces the dreamer to a level and quality of psychic and spiritual energy unique to the images of this culture.

A useful way of experiencing the different levels of energy at which an archetype can manifest is by contemplating the different images these cultures have produced. And for this a large museum can provide a helpful starting point, by making it possible to move easily between the artifacts of various cultural epochs; to immerse oneself deeply in the Greek statues, for example, breathing in their form and quality, and then comparing this experience, the sense of being a David or Aphrodite, with that of being an Egyptian pharoah or divinity. After some practice the energy level of the Greek images becomes palpably distinct from that of the Egyptian images. It even becomes possible to feel the vibrations of the images resonating with the different energy centers, or chakras, of our being.

Sally's dream reflected a psychological invitation to relinquish her home on the valley floor along with its more body-oriented and personal perspective, so that she could ascend toward the transpersonal chakras. The dreams which followed confirmed and elucidated the nature of this process.

She dreamed she was in an Egyptian mystery temple, undergoing secret initiation rituals and practices. The focus seemed to be on the process of mummification. She felt the inside of her body being washed by some kind of liquid which sluiced through its emptied cavities, and felt a mineral being placed in the orifices. As this happened she knew that the entire ritual was related to ones practiced in the epoch of Atlantis.

At the time of this dream Sally had no conscious knowledge of Egyptian mummification techniques. But some research revealed interesting parallels between the practices of this ancient civilization and the dream images. According to the Greek historian Herodotus, the first stage of the mummification process involved the removal of all inner organs apart from the heart, which was considered the seat of intelligence. The organs were then carefully treated and preserved in canopic jars. The only organ which was not considered worth preserving was the brain, which was scraped out through a puncture hole made in the nose and discarded. The cavities of the body were then carefully washed out with palm wine and spices and filled with myrrh and cassia. The surface was rubbed with natron, a kind of crystalline salt which was also packed into the orifices. Its effect was to dry and harden the body. After many days the salt was washed away and the body annointed with juniper oil and rubbed with myrrh and cinnamon. It was then bandaged and moved to its final resting place in the coffins.

The whole process took between sixty and seventy days. After the coffins had been sealed, the mummy was ready for the ritual ceremonies of the opening of the mouth, the ears, and the eyes. These rites were performed in order to return to the deceased the use of the senses so that he or she would be able to respond to the questions which would require an answer in the next world, in particular those asked by the forty-two gods who sat in the Hall of Judgment. These rituals of the "opening" were also performed on the statues of dead kings, to confer on them a living power and wisdom which transcended the limitations of body-bound knowledge.

This information helped Sally to understand the "living" quality of the statues in her first dream, their synthesis of stone and spirit, earth and heaven. It also helped her to recognize the dream images of mummification as part of an initiation process whereby the individual was enabled to reach beyond the limitations of time and space, to relinquish identification with all personal body-bound perspective so that he or she might experience the transcendent reality, while simultaneously retaining a relationship with body and earth. For the body was cleansed, purified, and rendered immortal. It was not burned or destroyed.

These dreams connected Sally with considerable new reservoirs of energy. Initially she found it difficult, as usual, to contain this energy. Its power frightened her, and her fear reflected itself in the dream of a large black beetle walking across her bed. As it approached it grew in size, rapidly acquiring the proportions of a small dog. Frightened, she began to chase it out of the room, and finally managed to shut the door on it. But undeterred by her hostility toward it, the beetle tried to creep back under the door. Still fighting, Sally stuffed the thin crack with old material, and as she did so she found her hand covered with worms.

The ancient Egyptians regarded the beetle, the sacred scarab, as an image of self-creation. They believed that it reproduced itself parthenogenetically from the ball of dung it rolled between its front legs. Under the name of Khopri, the "one who came forth from the earth," the "becoming one," it was, from earliest times, equated with the creator god Atum and associated with the sun. In chapter 85 of the *Book of the Dead,* the Creator says: "I came into being of myself in the midst of the Primeval Waters in this my name of Khopri." (trans. Robert Thomas Rundle Clark, *Myth and Symbol in Ancient Egypt,* London, 1978, p. 40). Thus Khopri was understood as the manifestation of God which occurred at the beginning of the world and reoccurs each day as the sun rises over the horizon. Sally's dream reflected the fact that she was doing her utmost to resist her own process of transformation. Recognizing this filled her with shame as well as new courage to continue the climb to the village of the gods.

Following a further dream in which she was being examined on the meaning and structure of the pyramids, those architectural images of the transition between life and death, Sally dreamed that she was beginning to meet the Egyptian gods and goddesses. Thoth, the Egyptian guardian of hidden knowledge, was present. She was shown the place of Da'at on the Kabbalistic Tree of Life and was told that the process she was undergoing concerned the cleansing of the mirror of soul so that the secrets of the cosmos might be revealed to her. Finally, she was commanded to remain silent.

According to Kabbalistic teaching, the place of Da'at, also known as the place of knowledge, lies in the spiritual world, at the crossing between the psychological and the divine. It is also known as the dark mirror, the place of the Holy Spirit. Kabbala teaches that while the mirror is clouded, the individual's perspective is limited to the personal worlds of body and psyche. Only as the mirror clears through the sacrificial death of the personal perspective can we begin to know and experience the spiritual world. In order for the necessary energy to accumulate to enable this transformation to take place, the dream voice reaffirmed the need for silence, the need to contain these experiences, to avoid spilling their power by talking prematurely about them.

A few nights later Sally dreamed that Thoth lived at the threshold of initiation; that she was standing in the center of a figure of eight, itself a symbol of the place of initiation; and that the eye of Horus was the portal of this initiation.

To understand the significance of this dream Sally turned to the Egyptian myth of Horus and Seth. According to the ancient Egyptian cosmology of Heliopolis, there was, in the beginning, the creator god Atum, "he who came into being of himself," before heaven and earth were separated. By copulating with himself Atum produced the first divine twins: Shu, the air, and Tefnut, the moisture. The hand which Atum used to copulate with himself was personified as the female principle inherent in the creator. From Shu and Tefnut was born the second twin pair: Geb, the earth, and Nut, the sky. They, in turn, produced two more pairs: Osiris and Isis, and Seth and Nephys. Geb appointed his son Osiris lord of the earth, thereby provoking jealously in his brother Seth, who set about planning the destruction of Osiris.

One night Seth managed to entice Osiris into a coffin which he then flung into the Nile. The coffin floated out to sea and was finally washed up in Byblos, where it was eventually found by Isis, as it grew within a tree. She brought the body of her brother-husband back to Egypt, whereupon Seth got hold of it again and dismembered it. Isis searched the land for the pieces of Osiris and found them all except for his phallus. Piecing them together, she conceived a son, Horus, from the spirit of Osiris.

Horus was the first of the Egyptian gods to be born a child. His mother, Isis, spent long years protecting him from the perils of the earth and the vengeance of Seth. Slowly, like a human being, he grew and matured, acquiring adulthood through sad experience. The struggles with Seth, which seem to have begun as Horus reached adulthood, are the rites of passage which carried him toward the realization of his divinity and wholeness.

Though there are different versions of these Seth-Horus struggles, a basic theme and pattern prevails. Symbolized as a fabulous animal, Seth was considered to be the god of chaos, of confusion, drunkenness, abortion, death, destruction, sex, and passion; the disturber of divine order and the one who separates that which was united. The

Seth hieroglyph functioned as a determinative for words indicating concepts divergent from the normal order, in contrast to the falcon of Horus, which was used to indicate divine reality.

The primordial period before the time of Seth and Horus was known as the era without conflict. In one of the Pyramid Texts it is eulogized as the epoch

> *when no anger had yet arisen*
> *when no conflict had yet arisen*
> *when no confusion had yet arisen*
> *when the eye of Horus had not turned yellow*
> *when the testicles of Seth had not yet been made impotent.*
> (H. te Velde, *Seth, God of Confusion*, Leiden, Holland,
> 1977, p. 33)

Psychologically, this epoch of divine peace reflects the preconscious state of humanity, which according to myth ended with Seth's murder of his brother, Osiris. Hitherto Osiris, as lord of eternal becoming, had lived on the earth. But now he was forced to move to the underworld, the realm of the unconscious, while Seth, ruler of passion and chaos, ruled the earth and consciousness. The opposites of life and death, consciousness and unconsciousness, had been thus brought into being by Seth's act. The divine preconscious oneness had been severed.

The relationship between Seth and Horus passes through three phases: homosexuality, conflict, and finally reconciliation. It is during the homosexual phase, initiated by Seth, that the left eye of Horus—symbol of his capacity to see, to be conscious—is damaged by Seth and he, in turn, is robbed of his potency by Horus. However, amid their complicated sexual entanglements Seth unwittingly conceives by the seed of Horus, which Isis had placed on Seth's staple diet of lettuces (a vegetable considered to contain aphrodisiac properties).

According to one tradition it is Thoth, the great god of wisdom, peace, and judgment, who finally succeeds in separating Seth and Horus and calling forth the seed of Horus from Seth. It emerges as a golden disk, an eye on Seth's forehead, from where Thoth takes it as his crown. According to this version Thoth is thereby deified, his divine wisdom a product of the marriage of Seth and Horus, of light and passion. According to another version Thoth finds the separate parts of the eye of Horus torn out by Seth's sexual assaults and puts them together in such a way that the eye, the spirit of Horus, finds a new state of being, made whole and holy by having been integrated with the seed of the passionate, vital essence of Seth.

The Horus Eye, synthesis of conscious and unconscious, spirit and matter, is then offered by Horus to his father, Osiris, thereby helping him to attain new life. According to one of the Egyptian sources, a Coffin Text (c. 2250 B.C.E.), the Eye of Horus is regarded as a divine entity (Te Velde, p. 46). No distinction is made in this text between the Eye of Horus and the Eye of Ra. "When did this god come? Before the shadows were separated, before the natures of the gods were made" (ibid., p. 47). According to a Pyramid Text,* Ra, the creator and sun god, hears the word of the gods with the eye of Horus. In this sense the eye seems to enable God to behold and relate to His own creation, to know the cosmos as His manifestation. The Egyptian king, regarded as a living god, was revered as a representative of Horus, and is referred to in one Pyramid Text as Horus-Seth.

In *Her-Bak, Egyptian Initiate* (New York, 1978) by Isha Schwaller de Lubicz, a conversation occurs between the Sage and his disciple in which Horus is described as the word of God who takes

". . .consciousness and possession of the man in whom he is weaving the human Horus. It is thus that he incarnates in man, bringing the supreme awakening to those who are ready for it."

"Horus is given many names . . ."

"As many as the transient states between his quality as universal quickener and his realization in the man made perfect through what he has gained in the course of his existence. He is called Hor the remote as the Horus-principle in course of becoming. He is called Hor *remet.t* as "proceeding from man's members," and in this name he struggles with the enemy, the Sethian personality. . . ."

"But may I ask where Horus is seated in myself?" . . .

" . . . Our texts tell you that 'he rises from your vertebrae'; from the dual fire in them, that is. That 'he quickens your spiritual heart, opens your mouth and eyes to the Real'; that 'being realized in you and having at last stripped you of your transient names, freed you from the humanity that is in your members,' he will 'reveal your true face,' your

---

*The Pyramid Texts were inscribed on the walls of the inner rooms of pharoahs and queens of the Sixth Dynasty.

face of Maât [universal truth and order], and 'make you one of the KAS [essences] of universal Horus.'"

(pp. 226–27)

To find the Eye of Horus is to discover and know our true identity as the eternal Eye/I of God, who weaves in and through our earthly incarnations, passing through the gates of death and life, knowing both and bound by neither. For Its essence is the essence of the universe in which all once existed in preconscious harmony, from which all is born, and to which all seek in consciousness to return.

Inspired by her dreams, Sally went to Egypt. Arriving in Abu Simbel, Luxor, Dendera, and Abydos, she felt she was revisiting old and familiar places, returning to a childhood home. She felt a long-forgotten joy in Dendera, a sense of peaceful service in Luxor, and sadness beside one of the tombs in the Valley of the Kings. These ancient sites seemed to live for her on two dimensions—as ancient spiritual centers, and as half-remembered episodes from her own history.

In a skeleton one-room shack with a corrugated iron roof and a few basic pieces of furniture, she met Omm Seti, an old English woman originally known as Dorothy Eady, who had devoted her twentieth-century life to completing a life which she knew had been cut short three thousand years ago by her suicide. For the last twenty-four years she had lived in this small shack and taken care of the ancient Egyptian temple of Seti at Abydos, where, she believed, as a virgin priestess of Isis she had once dishonored and defied religious law by having an illicit love affair with the pharoah Seti I (1306–1290 B.C.E.). Apart from allowing her to complete an unfinished life, Omm Seti's memories of that ancient time also enabled her to make some useful contributions to Egyptology.

Lying on her metal bed in her simple home beside the temple, Omm Seti told Sally a little of her life:

I was born in Maidstone, England, the daughter of an English doctor. When I was six I was knocked unconscious by falling downstairs. When the doctor arrived he pronounced me dead and left to get my death certificate. But when he returned, he found me playing happily in my bedroom.

From then on the dreams began—dreams of my home in the sands. I used to tell my parents of these dreams and ask them if I could go home. Of course they did not understand what I was talking about.

When I was six I saw a picture of the temple of Seti at Abydos in a copy of one of my father's magazines. I looked at the ruined sections and cried out, "Who has broken my home?" Then I looked at the sand around the temple and asked, "Where is the garden?"*

For the remainder of my childhood and adolescence I had recurring dreams of Abydos. Mostly these consisted of pleasant images of the temple as my home, and made me long to return there from my English exile. But one of these dreams was a nightmare. In it I was lying on the floor in a back room of the temple. All I could see were the feet and hems of the priests' robes as they beat me with a rod.

When I was in my early twenties, I married an Egyptian and went to live in Cairo. For nineteen years that city was all I knew of Egypt. But in 1952 I decided to satisfy my longing to visit Abydos. In those days the roads and railway signs were only in Arabic—but when the train approached Abydos, although I could not make out the station sign I immediately recognized the landscape and was able to walk straight to the temple without asking for directions. The moment I saw it I felt I had arrived home.

Quite soon after my arrival I entered a small back room in the temple and recognized it as the scene from my nightmare. Perhaps it was then that I realized I needed to stay here, to finish the work that I had failed to complete in that earlier life. Once I made that decision the nightmare never returned.

On the bumpy drive back to Luxor Sally pondered Omm Seti's story, comparing this ninety-year-old woman's memories of ancient Egypt with her own. The knowledge that they had once lived in that time, the joy of returning there, and the sense of familiarity at certain sights were experiences common to both of them. But whereas Omm Seti had felt that her memories of Abydos and her love for Seti I called her to stay in Egypt, to live as much as possible as she had done three thousand years ago, Sally's memories seemed to impel her to leave this ancient home, taking with her the essence of the pharoahs and their esoteric wisdom and allowing it to expand her awareness beyond the personal and ephemeral and carry her into

---

*At that time archaeologists had not discovered the temple garden. But in 1956 it was found exactly where Omm Seti had said it was. For a more detailed account of Omm Seti's remarkable story, see The Search for Omm Seti: Reincarnation and Eternal Love (New York, 1987).

new dimensions of the eternal nature of individual, earth, and cosmic being.

Buddhism distinguishes between the concept of rebirth and trans-migration, claiming that since there is no such reality as an individual soul but only the universal being of the universe, there can be no rebirth of individual souls, only the transmigration of personality-entities, defined by their inability to recognize and unite with the one Being—Self. Complementing the idea of sequential lives is an idea which has increasingly received attention recently, that of par-allel lives—different aspects of ourselves acquiring different experi-ences and therefore different opportunities for unfolding by incar-nating contemporaneously.

Whatever the truth about the details of reincarnation, it does seem clear that a single life provides insufficient time and experience for the psychological and physical transformation necessary to realize our oneness with Self, quite apart from being unable to account for the differences of individual talent, circumstance, and life opportu-nity. But in the end only the experience of a past life itself can convince us of its reality. For once we have had such an experience, any attempt by another to regard it solely symbolically, merely as an image of an unintegrated aspect of soul, or to suggest that we might simply have tuned into a different fragment of human history, is likely to leave us unconvinced and unsatisfied.

Understanding one life as but a fragment of a more complex web of lives enhances our capacity to assume responsibility for the nature and events of each life. For instead of regarding painful and difficult circumstances merely as incomprehensible bad luck, or blaming others for the difficulties they may appear to bring to us, the expe-rience of reincarnation enables us to see each event and individual characteristic, physical as well as psychological, as a direct conse-quence and reflection of our doing and being in previous lives, and therefore as an opportunity for growth and healing in this life, an opportunity for learning rather than lamenting.

However, the concept of many lives can also be used to obstruct our own becoming. Once we are armed with such an idea it can be tempting to forget to take the beam out of our own eye before taking the mote out of another's; tempting to explain an antipathetic feeling toward someone as "karmic," evidence of some painful circumstance between ourselves and that person in a previous life, rather than as an indication that we need to undertake the harder, more uncomfortable work of looking within to see whether the antipathy reflects a negative projection, part of our own ugliness mirrored to us by way of another.

Fortunately, perhaps, the spontaneous way of psychological unfolding protects us to some extent from such temptations. For unless the exploration of past lives is forced or hastened through hypnosis, drugs, or intensive conscious research, reliable and regular access to these lives does not normally occur until we have allowed many of our own unpleasant corners of soul sufficient access to consciousness, withdrawn a sufficient number of negative projections to have made us alert to this danger.* For until a considerable amount of this work has been completed we remain too locked into personal and ephemeral identities to accurately sense our longer history.

When we have gathered together enough of our being to recognize its timeless reality, and are spontaneously visited by memories of other lives, these memories bring much more than simple knowledge of our history. They also bring psychic energy which, inasmuch as it is integrated into consciousness, enlarges and transforms the experience of our soul, the world, and this earth life. For, as always, in remembering we psychologically re-member.

Although Sally's weeks in Egypt awoke in her, almost daily, many fragmented memories of a previous life, each enabling her to integrate new facets of her being, it was not until the last few hours before she left that she realized the psychological value of reconnecting and owning a previous life. She was sitting on the edge of a high hard bed in one of the somewhat dilapidated rooms of an old colonial hotel in Cairo. She had finished packing her bags for the return flight and was now reflecting on the inner events of the last few weeks. Amid the many flashes of remembering—the familiar statues, wall carvings, and contours of rock—one moment seemed to contain more power than the others. It had happened in the temple of Luxor, and the event not only provided insight into an episode of her past; it radically transformed the experience of her present.

She had been one of the first tourists to arrive at the temple gates that morning. The sun had barely risen and was not yet strong enough

---

*Of course, if past-life therapy is conducted with respect for the cathartic opportunities inherent in remembering past wounding, given and received, it can significantly facilitate the meeting and healing of our buried pain. For a detailed account of such work, see Roger J. Woolger, *Other Lives, Other Selves* (New York, 1987).

to burn away the cool mist which hovered around the ancient walls and pillars. As she stood outside the massive stone gates, tears came into her eyes. They came so fast that she noticed them before she was able to identify their cause. They were not tears of sadness, but more tears of remembering. To Sally they felt like the tears of returning to an ancient home, a long-forgotten place containing many gentle memories.

Entering the outer courtyard of the temple felt like coming home from an endless, lonely exile. But it was not until she entered the inner sanctuary, a small room at the core of the temple, that the remembering came in images. Standing alone in the semidarkness, surrounded by dank stones and carvings, she felt the being of a priestess arising from within her—one among a cohesive community of priests and priestesses dedicated to mediating between spirit and earth. These were men and women who had sacrificed everything personal so that they might serve the divine spirits, conveying their essence and will to those outside the temple and, at the same time, refining their own bodies and souls.

But this memory of mediating between the world of the gods and the world of matter and form did not move her as much as that of being a member of a community devoted to this end. For the first was not essentially different from her work in this twentieth-century life. But the feelings awakened by the second, the image of being a member of a temple priesthood, touched one of her rawest places.

Since early childhood Sally had felt alone with her interests and passions, often unbearably alone and out of tune with the excitements and aspirations of those around her. In the course of years of depth analysis, she had been helped to distinguish between the essential aloneness of being and the neurotic aloneness which she had unconsciously acquired to protect herself from her fears and wounds, the aloneness which severed her from her soul. Analysis had largely released her from this neurotic loneliness, this armored isolation. But it had left untouched a third kind of loneliness—that associated with feeling that her task in this life was essentially a lonely one, unsupported by the physical presence of like-minded people.

Remembering a time, another life, in which she had been surrounded and supported by a community dedicated to doing the kind of work she now did alone, gave her new courage and confidence; new strength to continue and deepen this work. The knowledge that she had once enjoyed the community warmth she now lacked seemed to lessen, even dissolve, the aloneness of this life. She felt that this living community to which she had once belonged was not merely a part of her history but was in some way still accessible to her. She felt the presence and vitality of its members, without knowing whether they were now incarnated in earth bodies or living at other levels of existence. In fact, knowing this seemed unimportant. What mattered was the experience of the immortal connection between them and between all whose lives were devoted to reconnecting earth and spirit.

It was a different Sally who boarded the plane at Cairo Airport that night. She had arrived in Egypt feeling about as old as her physical body. She left feeling that she was not thirty-one, but someone over four thousand years old living in a thirty-one-year-old body. This vastly increased time scale gave new proportions to many feelings and events in her life—things which had once loomed large now seemed small, dwarfed by the millennia. It was not that they had become less significant, but they had lost their power to threaten her. For her consciousness had expanded so much in that brief moment in the temple that many of the tidal waves of her life now appeared no larger than ripples.

An expanding scale of perception is one of the barometers of our own unfolding. Time appears to shrink as our souls increase in breadth and depth. Just as a young child may manage to wait an hour for something, and an adult a year, so one who has felt the breath of former lives may have the patience to wait a lifetime.

Space diminishes in the same way. Once human beings experienced the village pump as the core of their universe and were frightened to venture beyond it. Gradually the sense of universe expanded to embrace county, then country. A national consciousness was born. Now, perhaps too slowly for global well-being, national consciousness is being gradually superseded by world consciousness—the awareness of the community of individuals and nations and their interdependence with the earth.

Remembering former lives, particularly when this is accompanied by the knowledge that some of those with whom we shared earth experiences no longer live on earth, brings with it a sense of galactic and even, in some cases, intergalactic community. It brings the knowledge that there are many different dimensions of being, worlds other than earth in which we can live and become. And that each is indissolubly linked to all the others, so that the inhabitants of one have not only a responsibility but a necessity to think, feel, and act in tune with the rest.

Chapter Eight

NO TURNING BACK

Orpheus was so skilled a musician that when he sang and played the lyre the whole of nature was entranced. All creatures would follow him; even trees, plants, and stones were drawn to the beauty of his music.

He fell in love and married the nymph Eurydice. One day, as she was trying to escape the attentions of Aristaeus, Eurydice trod on a snake, which bit her leg, and she died.

Overwhelmed with grief, Orpheus ceased to sing and play and moved through his days in sadness and silence. Finally he went in search of Eurydice. When he reached the gate of the underworld, guarded by the watchdog Cerberus, he played his lyre so beautifully that he was allowed to enter.

The inmates of the underworld were as entranced by his music as the inhabitants of the upper world. So Hades and Persephone granted him the favor of allowing him to recover Eurydice, on the condition that he lead the way without looking back at her until they reached the upper world.

So together they set out on the journey from the underworld, Orpheus leading and Eurydice following behind. For a long time Orpheus managed not to look back at his beloved bride. But as he saw the first light of the upper world he could not refrain from turning round to see her face. Instantly she turned into a wraith of mist and vanished into the underworld.

After the dying, the sacrifice of each attachment, identification, possession, and security, each thing onto which we had projected a portion of our well-being, there follows the mourning. Long hollow days of sadness. An empty pool of life.

While other emotions—passion, desire, anger, and hate—spontaneously dissolve when we are willing and able to withdraw the psychological projection which gave them life and/or honor, the wound from which they protected us, the depression which permeates the soul in the wake of the sacrifice of ego attachments can feel interminable. It shrouds the days and nights with low, dark, windless clouds from which no rain falls and through which no sun shines. All outer support has gone—social and professional structures which once offered support and security; friends with whom to share joy and pain; lovers providing intimacy and human love; home and family; even the sense of meaning and purpose. In their place a heavy unknowing, a dark and homeless being.

And as the sacrifices and losses drain the soul, they also drain the body, depleting its vitality, undermining its resilience, weakening its immunity. For body and soul, as we have seen, are not independent realms, but different manifestations of one being. An empty soul soon reflects itself as an empty body.

So this time of mourning, essential and unavoidable, is nevertheless a risky, even dangerous episode of the journey. It is a liminal time in which old sources of energy, those dependent on attachments to ephemeral things, people, and situations, have dissolved and the new ones are still insufficiently accessible to consciousness. It is tempting in this darkness to look back, to turn to old supports. But the unfolding life of soul is a river which cannot flow backward. Of course there are many moments in the journey of becoming when consciousness turns around to recover and remember unhealed wounds and buried psychological attributes. Jung referred to these turnings as "reculer pour mieux sauter"—a turning back in order better to go forward. But the overall pattern of the journey does not turn back.

To hold onto something when its time has passed or inhabit a level of consciousness we have outgrown is to step aside from the river of our becoming. Initially it may feel good, even joyful, a safe respite from the days of pain and sadness. But quickly the ease and security lose their peace and become prison bars. For just as a child soon feels irritated if she returns to her mother's arms when she is able to walk, so does an adult who returns to outgrown ways in flight from the pains and fears of a new stage of becoming. We feel imprisoned and depressed, cut off from the life promised by the next stage of our unfolding, and angry with those who have colluded with our regression.

But it is not only the loss of freedom, inevitable in every turning back, which makes such a choice ultimately untenable and unsatisfactory. It is also because each new step in individual unfolding can only occur by way of a death. And once this death has occurred the energy locked in the old pattern does not spontaneously come to life again in that form. When the infant's umbilical cord is cut it cannot be recreated except by contrived and artificial means. And the same is true of every umbilical cutting throughout our lives. Even if only a small part of our being, a vanguard, undergoes the death which permits a new birth, that vanguard will have cut the ties to the old order, and no amount of nostalgia or fear will bring it to life again in any organic or ultimately satisfying form. The only creative possibility after such a dying is to allow and help the rest of our being to catch up with our vanguard.

After the big death—the final renunciation of ephemeral things and situations as the source of our fulfillment, security, and well-being—body and soul have been so sensitized by the transformative touch of Self that turning back is perilous. For the psychic energy which once expressed itself through such emotions as anger, hate, and desire without any undue harm to the body will damage and even destroy the body once it has been sensitized and refined by the fires of Self.

In certain (fortunately rare) circumstances this same principle of no turning back applies even if the return is not prompted by nostalgia or fear, but rather by conscious or unconscious recognition that we need to turn back in order to experience something we neglected to experience earlier; to re-member a part of our being, without which we cannot usefully travel onward.

If, for example, someone has done a great deal of disciplined meditative and spiritual work and a part of her soul has been sufficiently sensitized by the influx of high spiritual energy to have radically transformed her physical body, this body might not be able to withstand the integration of those coarser parts of soul denied by the individual in her single-minded pursuit of spiritual development. In other words, if the fires of the spirit are encouraged too strongly before an adequate descent into the depths of being, an adequate finding and integration of our earthly nature, spiritual practices might forge a body which, after many years, is unfit for such a journey of remembering, too refined and delicate to withstand the cruder energies still locked in the unconscious; too one-sided to realize in this lifetime its own wholeness.

Elisabeth Haich, in her autobiography, *Initiation* (trans. John P. Robertson, Palo Alto, Calif., 1974), tells of such a tragedy. Her story is a dramatic reminder that if we pursue the spirit prematurely, before having honored and allowed our own psychological becoming, found, enjoyed, and suffered our raw instincts and the earth on which we stand, we might jeopardize our capacity to do so in this life.

"If you want to achieve true knowledge," I tell him, "you must first learn to know yourself. You have to know *what you yourself are*. When you come to know yourself, you will discover that all the truths of the universe are concealed within your own being. Thus through this self-recognition you will get to know all the secrets of the world. First solve the great puzzle of our sphinx, that of man himself! . . ."

"I'm supposed to learn what I am? I've known that for a long time! Why is that supposed to be such a great mystery? But it seems to me, oh queen, that *you* don't know what I am, and so *I* am telling you: I am a man!" . . .

"I know very well that you're a man . . ." I answer him. But I can't even finish my sentence because the red-haired giant interrupts me impolitely: "It seems to me, queen, that you not only don't know I'm a man, but that you don't even know *what a man is*. I'm not a priest and can't read people's thoughts the way you can, but I know women, and I can see something you don't know at all—or else you've forgotten it—and that is what you are! You don't know you're a woman! How do you think you can try to teach me the inner secrets of man and the universe if you don't even know this simple fact that everybody else can see? . . . I am a man, and my other half can only be a woman who gives me complete and perfect happiness. For such a woman I would gladly lay down my life!"

I feel in my body a warm rush of blood that reaches my head. In the face of such a way of thinking I am completely powerless. How can I explain to him that the earthly happiness he is seeking in a woman is only transitory and unable to satisfy his immortal soul? . . .

.   .   .   .   .

"Look," I say, trembling, "it hasn't made any sense at all for you to come here to see me, because we just don't understand each other. We just can't get on together. I want to help you rise to the spiritual plane, and you want to drag me down to the level of the body. It hasn't made any sense at all to go through all this trouble. Go back to your homeland in peace, and we'll never meet again!"

At these words, the blood rushes to his head. His face, his neck . . . the whole man becomes dark red, so dark his hair seems lighter than his skin. His eyes flash like glowing embers, and with a shock I see his whole spiritual body turning into a powerful flame. Then, without my having time to defend myself, he seizes my arm, holding it as if in iron tongs, pulls me to his mighty breast, embraces me, pushes my head backward, presses his mouth to my lips with such force that I lose my breath. Then he kisses my face, my neck and my lips again, and in between his burning kisses, he whispers hoarsely: "So you don't want to see me any more? But *I* want to see you, and we'll meet again . . . we'll meet again."

As I saw his wild face coming close, I felt a wave of deathly panic. I wanted to push him back and get away, but as he locked me in his mighty arms and pressed his burning hot mouth upon my lips, all my inner being caught his fire. I lost control over myself, and without resistance I gave into the overpowering feeling of pleasure and delight that sprang up out of my fright and swept through me. Now I realize I love him . . . have loved him from the first moment . . . with all my body and soul . . . with my whole being I love him passionately and I always will!

The fire overwhelms me as if coming forth from a gigantic volcano. Hot flames sweep through me . . . devour me . . . my backbone feels like a bridge of glowing embers, holding seven burning torches. But now I'm no longer in the immovable axis of my spinal column, no longer in the midpoint from which my true *self* radiates the fire of life. On the contrary, my consciousness has fallen into my burning body, and sparkling, crackling, flashes of lightning race through my veins . . . through my whole being. All my nerves are aglow, all my thoughts blotted out. They're burning out my consciousness . . . annihilating me . . . Then I black out and everything disappears. . .

. . . . .

I lie on my knees before Ptahhotep.

I do not speak. He understands my unspoken words, even when I am silent. . .

"Father of my Soul, save me! Take this fire out of my body, give me back my freedom! I cannot and will not go on living this way. . .

"I lost myself, I am destroyed, I no longer have any control over myself, I can't think any more what I'm doing; my thoughts control me and split my head apart.

"Help me, Father of my Soul, help me back to the heavenly heights where spiritual clarity, purity and freedom reign. Give me back my wings so that I may fly again with you on high like the creative power of God, the divine hawk Horus, who flies through the universe creating new worlds."

.   .   .   .   .

. . . But I hear no answer. . . .

.   .   .   .   .

I return to the palace knowing only one thing for sure—that I *must* die. . . .

But I can't! I can't die! I must go on carrying within me the fire that's burning me up and destroying my nerves. I can't flee from myself. When I lie down completely exhausted to seek relief and rest a bit, I feel as if a mountain were weighing down upon my breast. I can scarcely breathe. Before my closed eyes I see blinding fire and flames, red flickering flames like the hair of the strange man . . . like the shabby mane of the lions. . .

The lions!—Yes, the lions, I will go to them.

And I'll dress myself as if preparing for a chariot ride.

The keeper lets me go to the lions, because he knows that ever since my initiation my father has allowed me to go out riding with the lions alone.

I go to my lions. They greet me with lowered head and with wrinkled nostrils. They smell a strange scent about me; they notice a strange and foreign emanation clinging to me. I go to Shima and stroke his head. Shu-Gahr lets out a loud growl, slowly drawing himself up ready to leap. Rage and jealousy blaze in his eyes, and the instinct of self-preservation awakens within me. I hurl my will against Shu-Gahr just as I used to guide him with my will-power during our chariot rides. But with a shiver of horror I realize I can't hurl my will any more. My will is lame and dead, and the lion leaps. . . .

Suddenly a great indefinable power draws my consciousness in some direction and I awaken. I'm lying on a sarcophagus and don't feel my body.

(pp. 324ff.)

Inasmuch as we fear, deny, and reject the flaming power of the lions within our souls, or any of our other animal instincts, they become our enemy. Not because they are inherently hostile but because, in being rejected by consciousness, they have been deprived of the opportunity for their own becoming, for their integration into the whole order of being. They have become outcasts, wild beasts to be caged up or allowed to roam in the wilderness, removed from relationship to the community of soul.

For a while Elisabeth Haich, in her Egyptian incarnation, was protected from the wrath of the lions by her innocence. But this same innocence kept her out of touch with her own female body, her womanly instincts, her sexuality—all that would connect her with body and earth. Without this half of her being she would never have been able to realize the wholeness that we are, to experience her oneness with creation. Her fall from the rarified air of the spirit into the chthonic pits of passion was a violent and destructive one. But it does not need to happen this way, provided we can consciously turn toward our instincts and passions, voluntarily accept and admit them into consciousness.

As more people are able to meet and integrate their own wild animals, to invite them into consciousness rather than barricade them in the unconscious wildernesses of soul, the transformation of animal nature will be felt not only within our souls but on earth itself. The instinctual capacity of animals to respond and react to the psychological states of those around them is well known: the cat who spontaneously moves toward certain people, the horse who bites whenever a particular man approaches. As we love our own inner animals, ceasing to project our unhealed relationship to our own instincts onto earth animals, they will be able to respond to us with a new gentleness. For animals, like all earth things, are hungry for their becoming. But being without human individual consciousness, they are, to some extent, dependent on us for their unfolding. Just as we are, in part, dependent on them for access and relationship to our instinctual wisdom.

Chapter Nine

GROWING OUT OF PAIN

Agnes turned. Her face was red-brown against the green, windy day. "Lynn, what do you believe in?" . . .

"Well, I believe in being honest."

Agnes laughed softly. She placed a small rock on the earth in front of me. "Go on," she said. "What else?" . . .

I went on to describe to her all of my important political and ethical values. By the time I had finished, there was quite a large mound of rocks.

"What does that mean?" I asked, indicating the pile.

"Those rocks represent each of your beliefs. There is the hoop of the world and the hoop of the self. Your hoops are like nests that surround you—very comforting. But you must recognize the existence of such safe nests. You must see that you sit on those rocks as if they were eggs and you were the mother hatching them. You must see that you are not free because you will never leave your nest of self-ignorance." Agnes pointed to the rocks. "There is your nest. You can spend the rest of your life hatching that if you want to. Those eggs will be the boundaries of your experience."

She toed the edge of the rockpile with her moccasins. "There is one egg that you would do well to hatch—one that is in harmony with the Great Spirit. It is the sacred rock at the center of the hoop. Hatch the sacred rock and you will hatch the queen bird that rips her talons through all the barriers to perception. Whether you believe me or not, hatch the idea that the hoop of the self is also the hoop of the universe. For you are the queen bird that soars on forever, limitless, and have no boundaries. Only the queen bird builds a true nest, without separations."

(Lynn V. Andrews, *Medicine Woman*, San Francisco, 1981, pp. 83–84)

With progressive loss and sacrifice the depression deepens. And since there is no going back, lest, like Lot's wife, we be turned to stone, deprived of the vitality which depends on flowing with our river, we must move on. But where to? In the dark hollows of depression it is not easy to hear the answer. For all around is death and dying, the disintegration of an old order of being which appears to offer few clues to the new.

Fortunately, as the depression intensifies and soul becomes correspondingly emptier, cleansed of ephemeral attachments, it also becomes correspondingly more receptive to the core of light and love which is Self. Meditative practices of quietly inviting the presence of Self, merging with this Being, become increasingly rich and satisfying, for the veil separating individual consciousness from its Self, burned thin by the flames of psychological transformation, now approaches its final dissolution.

As this happens, we may perhaps find new meaning in these lines from T. S. Eliot's poem "Ash Wednesday":

> *Although I do not hope to turn again*
> *Although I do not hope*
> *Although I do not hope to turn*
>
> *Wavering between the profit and the loss*
> *In this brief transit where the dreams cross*
> *The dreamcrossed twilight between birth and dying*
> *(Bless me father) though I do not wish to wish these*
> *   things*
> *From the wide window towards the granite shore*
> *The white sails still fly seaward, seaward flying*
> *Unbroken wings*
>
> *And the lost heart stiffens and rejoices*
> *In the lost lilac and the lost sea voices*
> *And the weak spirit quickens to rebel*
> *For the bent golden-rod and the lost sea smell*

Quickens to recover
The cry of quail and the whirling plover
And the blind eye creates
The empty forms between the ivory gates
And smell renews the salt savour of the sandy earth

This is the time of tension between dying and birth
The place of solitude where three dreams cross
Between blue rocks
But when the voices shaken from the yew-tree drift
* away*
Let the other yew be shaken and reply.
Blessèd sister, holy mother, spirit of the fountain, spirit
of the garden.
Suffer us not to mock ourselves with falsehood
Teach us to care and not to care
Teach us to sit still
Even among these rocks,
Our peace in His will
And even among these rocks
Sister, mother
And spirit of the river, spirit of the sea,
Suffer me not to be separated

And let my cry come unto Thee.
        (*Collected Poems 1909–1962*, New York, 1970,
                                    pp. 94–95)

   In this period, consciousness tends to oscillate somewhat unpre-
dictably between emptiness and fullness, between mourning the
renunciation and being filled with the serenity of the All, the I AM.
At the same time, ordinary life becomes increasingly difficult. Due
to the thinning of the veil between soul and body, the accelerated
influx of spiritual energy rapidly refines the soul, increasing its sensitivity and therefore inevitably the sensitivity of the body. Divested
of the relative psychological autonomy provided by identifying with
a separate ego personality, and without as yet the new identity of
Self, we become particularly vulnerable, tending, like sponges, to
absorb the atmosphere of whatever situation in which we find ourselves. If this is a spiritual one, we are nourished; but if, as is more
usual, it is characterized by the coarser energy frequencies of most
ordinary social and professional contexts, we are depleted and exhausted. For the emotional energy which constitutes much of twen-

tieth-century life (which forms the bulk of the content of most movies, television shows, and everyday conversation), the whole gamut of pleasure and pain, sympathy and antipathy, subjects the transformed but still unshielded body and soul to stresses they are too sensitive to withstand at this moment of their becoming.

Whereas prior to the work of the fire the experience of another's anger, for example, may be unpleasant; we usually have our own anger or patterns of denial and dissociation with which to deflect or ward off many of the psychic spears inherent in all violent emotion. But after the work of the fire, after suffering our own wounds as well as renouncing the ego attachments which spontaneously give rise to defensive anger, the old psychic skins have been removed, leaving us relatively defenseless.

Such a time, after the death of ego orientation and before union with the invulnerable sensitivity of Self, requires that we live a somewhat reclusive life and, like a caterpillar, honor the need to enter the chrysalis so that our delicate wings can unfold, safe from rough winds.

Though Western culture does not recognize chrysalis time, other cultures have done so. Indian tradition acknowledged the need for a time of withdrawal and introversion after completion of parental responsibilities; a time to go into the forest to find the Self. Today, in advanced industrialized cultures, many go into the forest before their chrysalis time, fleeing from Self rather than finding it. But some know and await the right time; first suffering, enjoying, and claiming their earthly nature, owning their existence as ordinary members of a human family, so that when the call comes, they can hear its truth and leave the outer world for the stillness of the trées.

Honoring chrysalis time often means withstanding the collective disapproval and condemnation it provokes. For those who do not know this time, who do not recognize its necessity for human as well as caterpillar becoming, tend to subject those heading for the forest to much misunderstanding and criticism, labeling their acts as irresponsible, a betrayal of society—a move, in short, of the utmost selfishness. And there is no way of proving to others the appropriateness of this retreat. Indeed, the wish to do so is more likely to reflect a desire to protect ourselves from our own unhealed critical subpersonalities, or from residual dependence on outer approval due to an incomplete realization of our inner truth, than from any impulse to awaken others to the reality of chrysalis time.

For Sally the chrysalis period did not take place all at one time but spread itself out over a number of years, during which she would feel the need for many relatively short periods of silence, sometimes not longer than a day, sometimes three or four days, in which she would leave her urban work and move to the solitude of a log cabin in northern Maine.

During one such period, sitting crosslegged on the stony bank of a small pond, awed by the silence of the forest in front and the strength of the hills behind, Sally felt her depression even more keenly, highlighted by nature's peace with itself. There seemed to be nothing in her life now: no friends who could understand her experience; no warm arms to hold her; no daughter. . . . She smiled despite herself as she noted this, for though she missed Rachael since she had left for college, she recognized and was grateful for the continuing strength and vitality of their relationship, for its honesty, and for the joy of watching Rachael walk her own path. For a moment these thoughts warmed Sally, but soon the depression returned and with it the litany of vacuums which had come to characterize her life.

As she sat there in the cool spring air, feeling the damp, newly melted earth beneath her boots, she wondered whether she had taken the wrong path. Was the analytic process a mistake, or had she misread the signs and lost the flow of her river? She wanted to call her analyst in London, the woman whose gentle wisdom had supported her during previous crises of becoming. But a telephone was a long way from this stony pond edge, and London even farther. So she sat still, comparing the joyful spring busyness of the birds to her own emptiness.

A few feet away from her a frog croaked. And not far from it, on the newly melted water, two more frogs were carousing with each other. They had been engrossed in this activity when she had arrived over an hour ago, but had stopped, frightened by the unusual presence of a human being. Now they had resumed their play, seemingly indifferent to her silent presence. She watched their antics, unsure whether they were courting or grooming each other, or merely playing. Whatever it was, they were fully absorbed in each other.

She found herself entering their cavorting bodies, finding and feeling their slippery frogness and from there spreading out into the quiet cold water, into its depth and expanse; then descending into the earth, merging with its dark weight, feeling her individual body as but a cell of her greater earth body. She breathed deeply, enjoying the one breath moving between mother and child. She felt the presence of Earth herself responding to her silent awakening, greeting her attention and experiencing their union. And she felt a new shame at all her inconsiderations toward this Earth goddess—her use of toxic cleaning agents, all of which poisoned this great and patient being, and the toxic chemicals she had subsidized each time she ate nonorganic food or bought synthetic clothing. She lay face down on the grass, breathing in the earth smells, and apologized for her ignorance, and asked that she might hear Earth's own needs for healing and becoming.

As she lay she felt the sun warming her back and inviting her to greet it as she had the earth. She sat up, feeling the heat melt her boundaries as it was melting the last hints of winter from the forest floor—melting them until there were no more to melt and she was released to feel the sun as well as the damp forest floor as inseparable expressions of her Self. Amid her joyful return to the oneness of the universe, she remembered Jung's final sentence in his autobiography, referred to in the dream which had heralded her inner journey: "In fact it seems to me as if the alienation which so long separated me from the world has become transferred into my own inner world and has revealed to me an unexpected unfamiliarity with myself." She realized that, for her, the "unfamiliarity with myself" emerged as her I gradually dissolved its identification with the ephemeral Sally and expanded to find itself as one with the source of creation, one with the Being of life and love.

Without losing her relationship with the uniqueness of her physical body and her own individual journey, Sally reconnected in that moment to the Easter experience seven years earlier which had first awakened her to the shift of identity from Sally to the I AM. And in contrast to the first experience, she realized now that this shift had come to stay; that though she would probably lose it many times in the future, the radiant joy of union with Self had become her new home, one to which she would always remember to return. She understood also that though she would be free at any moment to travel into other perspectives to identify with her body, personality, or individual soul, these were merely vehicles she had chosen for herself to enable her to journey toward a deeper experience and understanding of the Self that is simultaneously individual and universal, earth as well as spirit. Moved by this knowing, she reflected on Sally for a moment and smiled as she imagined the fun she would now have accompanying her through her future physical and psychological adventures.

Late that afternoon, as the sun was setting, a cool wind moved through the forest, telling of the approach of night. Sally got up and began to climb back to the cabin on top of the hill. As she walked, she remembered the dream she had received at the beginning of the period of dying, in which she met the woman who was able to travel at will between Earth and the other planets, able, it seemed, to move freely between different levels of consciousness, to explore and enjoy a disembodied as well as an embodied existence.

As she entered the cabin she smelled faint vestiges of the morning's burned toast and noticed that her body was hungry. With slow delight she washed and cut up a generous selection of vegetables and lovingly prepared a large soup. Eating it together with some warm, unburned toast and tahini, she felt grateful to the earth and her body for giving her the opportunity to travel out of pain into oneness with the cosmos. And she noticed that soup had never tasted so good, nor felt so sacred.

After cleaning the cabin she found herself wanting to return home. Her time in this remote and secluded beauty seemed to have reached its conclusion, and she was eager to enter earth business again.

It was dark by the time she reached her small city home, but there was sufficient moonlight for her to see the envelope pinned to her door even before she had parked the car. She knew it was from Chris, whom she had not seen for nearly four months, not since he had said that there was no space in his life for their relationship. Reading his cryptic note about wanting to see her unleashed the love which had rarely been out of reach since their relationship had begun over five years ago. She was still suffused by it when he walked through the door the following evening.

He looked different, had lost a little of his beauty and acquired more lines on his forehead and some new ones between his eyes. He seemed tired and worn. No longer the man she had once been in love with, but unmistakably the man she loved.

He was hesitant, a little apologetic for having walked out of her life. They stood facing each other for a moment in the narrow hall, digesting the delight of being together. Then she reached for him. As they embraced she noticed how she hugged him with her body, enjoying his arms, the hungry pressure of his chest against hers, and also how she hugged him with her soul, feeling the overlapping of their love. She realized again how their bodies were separate and would always be so even during the next hour or so as they made love, but she knew that their souls could merge in love without Sally losing any of her recently realized sense of oneness with the universe, none of her I AM-ness; that, on the contrary, her realization of the I AM had only increased her capacity to love him both as he was this evening and as another I AM living on this earth.

Though their bodies were still quiet, their souls had already begun to make love, appreciating and drinking in each other, allowing their harmonious notes to create and amplify their song.

By the time they had moved to the bedroom and were lying on Sally's futon, memories of their months apart had faded into the delight of their present moment. He kissed her gently, tenderly, sensitive as always to her body language and the play between them. For a moment she wondered whether, after the experiences of the last two days, she would be able to or even want to respond erotically. But beneath his gentle love she soon discovered that nothing joyful had been taken away by her birth into the I AM. It had merely provided her with new choices, a new dimension of freedom. She could enjoy loving him with just her soul. Or she could also love him with her body, delighting in the particular opportunities for pleasure and love offered by bodies. That evening she chose to relate with all of her. And as she chose she experienced a delicious melting in the core of her body. Eagerly she welcomed him into her warm pulsating moistness, their hearts and eyes connecting in the creation and expression of love.

Afterward, as they lay together in the naked warmth of body, bed, and passion, as he gently kissed her lips in appreciation and gratitude for the love which was once again flowering between them, she realized that nothing had changed in his life. His other relationship was still there, and soon he would be leaving her bed, pulling on his socks, tucking his shirt carefully into his pants, ruffling his hair into some kind of order with his fingers, and walking out the front door. Once again she would hear his car drive away and know that he was returning to his other relationship. She remembered similar moments, many of them, when she had been in love with him, when she had found with him the I AM-ness she had now realized to be herself. She remembered the anguish as he left, the feeling that some part of her was being wrenched away with each parting step, the painful images of him with her.

Briefly she imagined the same pain would return tonight. But then she knew she was different now; knew and felt that her love for him was no longer confused by the desire for her own fulfillment, but lived free, able to delight in their being together but also to flourish when she was alone, even when she saw him with her.

Silently she thanked him for coming into her life as he had, incompletely, spasmodically. Thanked him for providing the beacon which had awakened her to the fulfillment of a love which is sufficient unto itself.

When, a few moments later, he began to extricate his body from hers and reach for his clothes she watched him, keenly hoping that the choices he was living were his stepping stones to Self.

It can be difficult to distinguish between union with Self and the spiritual pride of ego inflation if we merely listen to the words used to describe these two radically different psychological states. For a person going through a psychotic episode as well as one who has awakened to the I AM consciousness may both say of themselves, "I am God." But when the psychotic uses these words they express the identification of his ephemeral body and personality with Self, and may well contain the unspoken message "I am God and you are not," as well as the feeling that his experience of his divinity isolates him from others. When, in contrast, the ego identity is dissolved by way of one's relationship to the spontaneous unfolding of union with its source, the Self, the individual experiences his divinity as one with the divinity of every other person. Such an experience does not raise him above others (except in the sense that he has walked the human path a little further than some) but, on the contrary, awakens him to his essential identity with all people.

The death of ego separateness, which occurs spontaneously as the love and light of Self transforms all that is sacrificially placed upon its hearth by the re-membering work of consciousness, recalls, reverses, and unfolds the pattern of many creation myths:

In the beginning God created the heaven and the earth. And the earth was without form, and void; and darkness was upon the face of the deep. And the Spirit of God moved upon the face of the waters.

And God said, Let there be light: and there was light.

And God saw the light, that it was good: and God divided the light from the darkness.

And God called the light Day, and the darkness he called Night. And the evening and the morning were the first day.

(Genesis 1:1–5)

Some creation myths express the differentiation of the whole which gives birth to light and consciousness as the dismemberment of a primordial giant:

> *From the flesh of Ymir the world was formed,*
> *From his blood the billows of the sea,*
> *The hills from his bones, the trees from his hair,*
> *Out of his brows the blithe powers made*
> *Midgarth for sons of men,*
> *And out of his brains were the angry clouds*
> *All shaped about the sky.*
> (Esther Harding, *Woman's Mysteries, Ancient*
> *and Modern,* New York, 1972, p. 187)

A popular Chinese creation myth tells a similar story:

Born from the original Yin-Yang polarity, the primordial giant Pan Gu grew ten feet each day for eighteen thousand years, pushing the heavens away from the earth. When he died, the various parts of his body were transformed into the world. His breath became the wind and the clouds, his voice the thunder and his sweat the rain. His left eye became the sun and his right eye the moon. From his body issued the great mountains. His blood and bodily fluids became the rivers and the seas, and his nervous and venous systems became the layers of the earth. The fields were the transformation of his flesh, and the stars and planets developed from the hairs of his head. Metals and stones were the products of his teeth and bones. His semen became the pearls, and his bone marrow turned into jade. The human race developed from the fleas of his body.

These stories tell of differentiation, light, and consciousness being born through the sacrifice of wholeness. They express consciousness and oneness as alternatives. But the dissolution of ego identification and union with the infinite ocean of Self occurs not at the expense of consciousness but by way of it; not by drowning the light but by enhancing it, by unveiling the greater whole which underlies all forms and differences, yet without diminishing the capacity to discern and experience the differences. The cosmic giant whose death gave birth to earth and human consciousness finds life again by way of individual renunciation and dying.

This giant of a human being who comes to life by way of the sacrifice of ego identification is not a simple reversal of the creation myths, but rather a return which is simultaneously a new creation:

> *We shall not cease from exploration*
> *And the end of all our exploring*

Will be to arrive where we started
And know the place for the first time.
Through the unknown, remembered gate
When the last of earth left to discover
Is that which was the beginning;
At the source of the longest river
The voice of the hidden waterfall
And the children in the apple-tree
Not known, because not looked for
But heard, half-heard, in the stillness
Between two waves of the sea.
Quick now, here, now, always—
A condition of complete simplicity
(Costing not less than everything)
And all shall be well and
All manner of thing shall be well
When the tongues of flames are in-folded
Into the crowned knot of fire
And the fire and the rose are one.
(T. S. Eliot, "Little Gidding—1942," *Col-
lected Poems 1909–1962*, pp. 208–209)

Costing not less than everything, the act of becoming Self is a return to the endless space, the nothingness which is the seed of all, and consciously identifying with it, inhabiting it for the first time.

Whereas the birth of Self initiates us into an experience of Self, launching us on a long and intimate I–Thou relationship, union with Self dissolves all vestiges of separateness so that finally we recognize and feel our being as one with cosmic being. And it does so without diminishing our capacities for discrimination and discernment of personality and other human and earthly differences, but simply by reuniting the flame of individual Self with the cosmic fire, melting the I–Thou relationship into the I AM.

But this I AM experience does not mean that we have lost all individuality. For although we now recognize the illusion of individuality, and experience our soul as the one soul, our capacity to reflect and know this oneness is embryonic, infinitely small and weak compared to the pure reflectors of the One, such as Jesus Christ.

The transition from relating to Self to being Self is felt as a shift in the focus of energy from the heart to the crown of the head. Love, for example, no longer only flows from the heart but radiates from the eyes and from a still point above the head. In this process of transformation none of the heart love is lost. It merely becomes available at a new level of refinement, united with the light of wisdom. Rather than losing touch with one level of consciousness in order to move into another level, we become free to travel up and down a greater spectrum of consciousness, able to visit at will the heart or sexual centers, our body, and individual feelings, and always return to our universal home in Self. And we find the freedom to fully own and enjoy our bodies and unfolding souls without being overwhelmed by the limitations of consciousness, the loss of union with our source, which is responsible for emotional suffering.

The relationship between pain and consciousness—born mythologically in the garden of Eden with Adam's and Eve's eating of the forbidden fruit of the tree of knowledge, and recapitulated in each individual life with the separation from the preconscious oneness which gives rise to the birth of individual consciousness—finally dissolves when we enter again the garden of Eden and know it for the first time.

But since the awakening to paradisiacal consciousness occurs only when all identification with the personal has been relinquished, when everything has been sacrificed and we have found our being as simultaneously the being of every other person as well as the being of earth and stars, consciousness of suffering will continue for as long as any person, flower, or animal is in pain. But feeling another's lonely expulsion from paradise, her pain at her own incompletion, is different from personally suffering that pain. Whether the feeling takes the form of empathy or compassion, it does not conflict with the serene joy of union with Self.

Our capacity for empathy is a consequence of our capacity to acknowledge and suffer our own wounds. Inasmuch as we deny a pain within ourselves, we are likely to be too defended from it to feel a similar wound in another. Inasmuch as we have suffered our wounds, our feelings are opened to those similarly afflicted. Empathy, therefore, gives us access to the process and being of another by way of our own process and being. It can help others to feel less alone, less misunderstood in their pain, and therefore more able to honor and suffer it. But by itself empathy, unlike compassion, can comfort but cannot heal.

Compassion is one of the breaths of Self. It sees as well as warms, not only inviting the other to recognize her pain, but, by virtue of its source, spontaneously helping to heal this pain, to transform it in the fires of love and wholeness. Whereas empathy moves us into tune with the suffering of the other, depleting to some extent our own vitality, compassion, which is available only to the extent that the soul receives the flow of Self, nourishes the giver at the same time as it helps to heal the one in pain.

Relinquishing the I–Thou relationship to Self for the joy of the I AM occurs through a process of progressive relaxation. It involves a letting go of all levels of physical, psychological, and mental tension which created the once necessary illusion of our separate identity; the tension which enabled individual consciousness to mature to the point at which it could withstand the dissolution of its separate identity without dissolving itself in the process.

Each effort and struggle to hold on to anything instantly casts us back into the dualistic perspective and the suffering this inevitably contains. For the I AM is only accessible when we have relinquished all, removed all our psychological clothes and are able to stand as naked as Adam and Eve before they were cast out of paradise. Any emotion which arises at this stage—fear, desire, anger, or even depression—needs to be relinquished in the knowing that since a greater level of being and feeling is now accessible, it is uncreative to perpetuate a lesser one.

In the early stages of this transition from the world of emotional suffering to the world beyond, consciousness tends to oscillate rapidly and frequently between the two. So it is useful to remain alert to the distinction between dissolution and denial, to remember that soul unfolds not by way of rejecting itself (repressing uncomfortable emotions, for example) but by way of finding, integrating, re-membering, and only then by sacrificing. Where denial and dissociation persist, essential parts of our being remain imprisoned in the unconscious, not only out of touch with the possibility of transformation, but also creating a potential threat to consciousness. They appear to us in dreams and fantasies as the intruder in the night, the rapist, the murderer—the one trying to enter the house of our being, to gain admission into our inner community against the will of consciousness. Denial, therefore, impoverishes the soul, keeping it locked at one level of being and perpetuating hostility between conscious and unconscious, whereas sacrifice enriches and transforms soul. For only that which we consciously own can be sacrificed; and the act itself—the offering of the newly gathered energy to the fires of Self—allows the dying of one mode of being so that a new and greater one may unfold.

The complete relaxation into Self, this total renunciation even of emotion, can feel at first like a betrayal of everything which enabled Self to awaken into consciousness. It is particularly difficult for those for whom the larger part of their early psychological work revolved around learning to listen to, acknowledge, and allow emotions after years of denying and dissociating from them. For in the early stages of the journey to Self, emotions are, as we have seen, a vital and irreplaceable vehicle of becoming. They introduce us to who we are, rather than who we think we are or think we need to be. They are the raw material of our unfolding, the stuff of soul. And since listening to body and emotion, recognizing and integrating the projections they reflect, can take many years, decades, even lifetimes, we are likely, at least to some extent, to identify emotions with soul rather than recognize them as only one form in which soul can live and express itself—a form essential to one stage of human unfolding but a hindrance to the next.

Sexuality is a good barometer of which side we are standing on at this stage—denial or sacrifice. For if sexual energy has been repressed it will rise up, as we have seen, challenging the conscious attitude. But if the instinctual and erotic expressions of Self have been fully experienced, any sacrifice of sexuality enables this energy to ascend the different levels of being—becoming first warmth, then love, then the creative word before reaching its flowering as loving wisdom.

It was the instinctual chthonic energies of the snake which tempted Adam and Eve to reach for consciousness. The birth of human knowledge was bought at the cost of recognizing human nakedness—acknowledging our own separate, earth-bound nature. But, as the ancient Egyptians acknowledged by the emblem of the snake on the pharoah's crown and the Indians expressed in their Kundalini teachings, the snake energies which cast us out of the preconscious paradise are the same ones which can carry us to a conscious one. The feeling of the snake stirring in the bowels of our being and flowing freely, by way of soul, up the spine of soul to union with the spirit is an ecstatic experience in which each part of us is engaged and connected; each cell, feeling, image, and thought participating in a flow of joyful and vital serenity.

The free movement of the snake between different modes of being, between body and spirit, is one of the gifts of the long years of psychological exploration and integration. For soul, as the middle ground between the two poles of Self, earth and spirit, can be, as we have seen, a bridge or an obstruction to our capacity to hold hands with Self. When it is a bridge, new choices become available:

A snake slid up the drain this morning
as I stood beneath the shower.
Slipping from that dark deep hole,
it eased itself between my ankles;
began its wet ascent
to warm centers,
fresh interstices of flesh and soul.

At rest, for now, around my heart,
accumulating fire,
spine power,
I recognize a choice,
some ways for it to move:
an offering to you in love,
a sacrifice in word.

The choices created by the capacity for our energy to flow freely between the different centers may radically alter the way in which we relate. In sex, for example, physical arousal no longer needs to be released in orgasm, for the energy can as easily be invited to ascend to the heart center and released as love; or to ascend even further so that it may radiate out from the eyes as a healing and blissful light. The free movement of the snake, therefore, makes us self-sufficient, not because we cease to need anything but because we have everything. Freedom replaces compulsion.

Union with Self as the source of unlimited vitality and wealth also has consequences for how we learn and speak. Instead of paper and print, field and sky become our book, with each leaf and flower, each roaming bumblebee, each chance encounter or passage of the wind forming its words and sentences. This is a book that needs to be read not just with the eyes but with psychological limbs and fingers, nose and ears, with imagination and intuition, thinking as well as feeling. It invites our complete immersion, our silent contemplation, all the time showing us that earth words are too small, too crude, and too few to reflect this universal living language of light.

It can take many years of listening to body, soul, and spirit before the wordless creative language—the archetypal idea seeds—reveals itself within earth languages; many years before we can actively cooperate in creation through the use of this universal language. But sometimes glimpses of the nature and meaning of these creative possibilities come to us long before we are ready to make use of them. Sally's earliest such glimpse arrived in a dream:

She found herself with a man she had met a few times. As she looked at him his form and features peeled themselves away, revealing an unknown man. After a few moments his appearance also dissolved, and she found herself in the presence of the source of these ephemeral forms—a radiant being, without shape or sex, one whom neither time nor space had the power to limit or confine.

"Come!" The being commanded in the wordless words of the spirit. "I want to show you something."

Together they journeyed to the cradle of creation, the center of the cosmos, where the lesser light of the being fused with the greater light of its divine parent and illumined the place of the hidden mysteries. There she experienced the living language, the immortal and immutable vibrations which call the universal spirit into body and earth.

She was reluctant to leave this transcendent place, this home. But the being insisted she return. When they reached the frontier between the unchanging realm of light and the ephemeral images and forms of earth, it spoke again: "Those who have experienced the way and the truth of the living word may enable others to feel its presence and recognize its will."

Turning from the eternal, she looked at its myriad earthly appearances. And with the power of its word still resonating within her, she experienced with sadness the crude poverty of human language. For, bereft of union with their divine source, earth words tasted like husks within her mouth, like ash upon her tongue.

The opening verses of the Gospel of Saint John tell a similar story of the creative power of the living word:

In the beginning was the Word, and the Word was with God, and the Word was God.

The same was in the beginning with God.

All things were made by him; and without him was not anything made that was made.

In him was life; and the life was the light of men.

And the light shineth in the darkness; and the darkness comprehended it not.

(John 1:1–5)

The Living Word spoken of in the dream and the Gospel is as near and as far from the spoken word as Self from an individual body. To hear it is to have access to the source and mysteries of creation. The sacrifice of learning by way of earth words, written or spoken, is of course only a preparatory step toward such listening and hearing, though an essential one if it helps us to listen for the living truth within. However, it is a difficult step to take in our print-bound culture. Some have the wisdom to accept it voluntarily. Others, like Sally, have it forced upon them, years before even glimpsing the possibility of union with Self.

She had acquired the habit of always carrying a selection of books with her wherever she went, even if it was only to sit in the garden. For her hunger for understanding was so great that time without reading felt like time wasted. Her books provided her with many valuable insights. They also inspired her to meditate more, study more, even to ask more. Though they never satisfied her hunger for knowledge, they did serve to increase her appetite.

One morning, a few years before she entered analysis, she awoke in her London apartment to find she could not see. Her eyes seemed to be covered by an opaque veil. Frightened, she called a friend, who came and took her to an eye specialist. After examining her for some time the doctor confessed to being baffled by the condition, gave her some eye drops, and sent her home to rest.

The next morning the veil had thinned sufficiently for her to see, more or less; but when she tried to read, her eyes soon became bloodshot and felt as though they were filled with fine sand. She put aside her books and adjusted herself to an involuntary rest from learning. She went to the south of France for a vacation; swam, slept, and rested her eyes, imagining that she had overstrained them and that, in time, they would spontaneously heal. But when she returned home, three weeks later, and began reading again, the painful bloodshot condition recurred.

So she began a round of visits to different eye specialists. Some admitted to being as bewildered as the first doctor she had seen, and were honest enough to say so. Others diagnosed her condition as lacerations of the cornea and advised more rest.

One afternoon, after visiting yet another specialist and hearing yet another "I don't know," Sally was sitting in her apartment looking out of the French windows at the rose bed, idly wondering how flowers survived at all in urban air, when the thought came to her that perhaps she would never be able to read again. As the shock wore off and she began to digest this possibility, she was surprised to discover that the image of a bookless life, though disturbing and somewhat empty, also felt like a relief. She even touched a glimmer of excitement at unknown possibilities which might come to life in hitherto book-filled hours.

But the excitement soon faded as she began to live a bookless reality. For while her friends read or studied, absorbed in their private print worlds, she felt depressed, with nothing to do. She would look out of the window at the winter sky, or at her friends and remember the life she used to lead. Sometimes she went for walks. But often she just sat, aware more of what she was not able to do than of the possibilities of what she might do. She tried replacing books with music and spent hours listening to Bach and Mahler, but this soon palled, as did anything else she reached for in an attempt to fill the hours.

But then spring came, a particularly gentle, delicate spring, without fierce winds or residual winter cold, and Sally found herself leaving the city for the country to meander through woods and beside newly sown fields. During these hours, for the first time since her bookless life began, she ceased to feel that she was filling in time and became absorbed in a world she had never seen through the pages of a book—a world of animals, plants, and trees, all hungry, it seemed, for relationship with her and anyone else interested in listening.

And after each of these sojourns into nature's spaces she noticed a new interest in entering nonphysical spaces—her emotions, feelings, and thoughts, as well as the silent invisible realms accessible through meditation.

By the time that spring had passed into summer and the first hints of autumn were visible, Sally's hours, though still bookless, were no longer empty.

The shift in the source of knowledge from outer learning, books and teachers, to inner listening, observation, and reflection, makes possible the dying of the intellect and the birth of a new form of thinking, one which relies less on reasoning and more on a silent receptivity to the world of wordless thought. When Sally was seventeen, some years before the bookless period, she had been introduced to a little of what this meant, even though she had been too unconscious to make much use of the insight.

"Write me an essay on 'Serendipity,'" her tutor said as he gathered up his papers, signaling the end of her first tutorial for 'A' level English. Sally was too nervous, too in awe of this fiery redheaded intellectual whom she had chosen to prepare her for university entrance, to tell him she had no idea what "serendipity" meant, that she had never even heard of the word and therefore could not imagine how she could write a paper on the subject. So instead she just nodded her assent, while attempting to keep in check the panic rising within her.

The moment the apartment door closed and she heard him descending the stairs, she reached for the *Shorter Oxford English Dictionary* and read: "*Serendipity.* The faculty of making happy and unexpected surprises by accident." This did little to allay her anxieties about the essay, for though she now understood the word, her somewhat unstructured education had not prepared her to write papers on such abstract subjects.

However, her determination not only to get into the university of her choice but also not to look small in the eyes of her tutor impelled her to sit down immediately and attempt the project. Facing a new block of naked paper, she thought about things that might happen by chance, about other ways in which things might happen, about the meaning of chance . . . on and on, late into the night, until her brain ached from such unaccustomed exertion.

Finally, too tired to continue, she sat back, put down her pen and relaxed for a moment. Suddenly ideas began flowing toward her, insights and inspirations, answers to some of the questions her arduous thinking had dug up. Quickly she wrote them down. And they later formed the backbone of her paper. She largely abandoned the results of the hours of careful reasoning and intellectual thinking.

In writing about "serendipity" she had herself been serendipitous (a word not in the *Shorter Oxford English Dictionary*). By a happy accident she had discovered that true understanding does not come by way of intellectual thought; that while thought can explore the known, question and analyze it, its greatest gift is in revealing its own limitations, in taking us beyond intellectual thinking to the place of stillness where the mind can tune into the world of wisdom.

The wisdom born from contemplating nature, soul, and spirit reveals itself in direct proportion to the work of the fire. It is a wisdom which arrives silently, creeping up from behind, waiting until we turn around or within and awaken to the knowledge that we now see and understand things which yesterday were hidden. The process feels like veils being removed, leaving us sensitive to finer frequencies of truth. Suddenly, for example, the tree reveals its life body as well as its trunk and branches, a person her aura.

The return of individual consciousness to its Self—which permits this qualitative change in the depth and subtlety of wisdom—also feels like a progressive melting of the parameters of consciousness and being. Even the most solid of objects—our bodies, the earth— seem to breathe a new fluidity and life, becoming no less real or valuable, perhaps more so, but significantly less substantial and static. A sheet of glass, for instance, may cease to seem static and be "seen" instead as sand moving very slowly.

Merging with these changing forms and their unchanging essence, allowing the totality of being, will, feeling, and thinking to recognize its unity with the world and all that it contains, is to fall in love. Not with anyone or anything, but directly—to stand in love and as love, feeling its eternal waters rising through us until they become us, transforming our being into a spring of life from which all may drink and which none can deplete, a spring which the vicissitudes of the ephemeral world cannot contaminate or divert.

> The man who sees Brahman abides in Brahman: his reason is steady, gone is his delusion. When pleasure comes he is not shaken, and when pain comes he trembles not.
>
> He is not bound by things without, and within he finds inner gladness. His soul is one in Brahman and he attains everlasting joy.
>
> For the pleasures that come from the world bear in them sorrows to come. They come and they go, they are transient: not in them do the wise find joy.
>
> But he who on this earth, before his departure, can endure the storms of desire and wrath, this man is a Yogi, this man has joy.
>
> He has inner joy, he has inner gladness, and he has found inner Light. This Yogi attains the Nirvana of Brahman: he is one with God and goes unto God.
>
> (*Bhagavad Gita*, trans. Mascaró, 5.20–24)

With the arrival of this kind of joyful serenity, the years of psychological and spiritual work in which we learned to recognize, follow, and feed our becoming reach a resolution. In this moment we experience the river of soul reaching its destination and silently slipping into the sea.

But the sense of relief and wholeness, the peace of reaching and becoming the ocean, also brings new questions, new unknowns. It is a turning point in which, as usual, it is necessary to relinquish old ways of working and being in preparation for the next round of becoming, to accept the death before realizing the birth. But the nature of this particular dying can be hard to recognize. For since ego's initial struggle and humbling in which it realized the existence of a will greater than its own, the will of soul, the "I" became accustomed to following its river, swimming with it through the sometimes treacherous waters of death and rebirth. And though this process was often painful and frightening, the river's existence was nevertheless something to follow. But when its waters disgorge themselves into the ocean, we lose a trusted guide and find ourselves adrift in a realm of seemingly unlimited possibility.

It took Sally some weeks before she recognized the nature and meaning of this change. Initially she was eager to rest after the long journey, delighted not to be on the move, and happy with the tranquil and joyful place at which she had arrived. But one morning, perhaps when she had taken all the rest she needed, she awoke with a desire to question and explore the new psychological place.

She lay in bed listening to the constant hum of the distant highway, crammed as always at this hour with commuters. Occasionally the tone was interrupted by the louder noise of a local car taking a child to school.

She snuggled further under her down duvet and watched a largish ant busying its way through her bedroom door. She wondered whether it would choose to climb across her floor-level futon and join her under the duvet. But this thought was soon interrupted by the question of what she wanted to do this morning, and tomorrow morning, and the mornings after tomorrow. For now that the pain and grief which had been her regular companions for decades had dissolved, replaced by a loving peace, there was no apparent psychological work inviting her attention, nothing to do, it seemed, until her first clients arrived later in the morning. She did not even need to rest, for the nights, no longer wrapped in pain, were once again available for sleep.

Leaving these questions hanging for a moment, Sally relaxed again into the soft down warmth and enjoyed the peace and joy which permeated this morning, as they did every morning. She reflected on the night's dreams and wondered again why they contained no indications of where she should be moving in her life, when they had always done so in the past. Recently they had been remarkably restrained, confining their messages to reflections of minor ripples in her days, moments in which she still wobbled unsurely between the old ways and the new. But somehow she knew that since the old I–Thou relationship to Self had dissolved into the union of I AM, the old ways of following had also dissolved. She continued to lie under the duvet. The ant had by now chosen not to climb over her, at least not for the moment, and had departed for a small corner of dust underneath the chest. The sun's rays had left the small side window and were now shining through the cracks in the peach-colored curtains. Soon it would be hot. She thought about getting up and drawing the blinds in the kitchen and study to protect what cool darkness had given them. But the questions kept her under the duvet.

And then it happened. The idea of choice arrived, shocking her into a new awakeness. Not the choice of whether or not to follow the will of her own becoming—the Thy Will or mine choice—which really had not felt like much of a choice for many years. But an entirely different kind of choice, a free choice in which it would be perfectly all right with her soul, with Self, whatever she chose. The kind of choice which is born from arriving home, from recognizing our unity with the universe, the trees and grass, as well as with each human being; the possibilities of choosing how and what to contribute to herself and therefore, since their interests were identical, to this world.

Moved by the playful opportunities as well as the responsibility implied by such freedom of choice, Sally lifted off the down duvet and walked toward the shower. But as she enjoyed the feel of the warm water cascading over her nakedness, the next question arose. If she had now arrived in a place of unlimited free choice, how could she choose? What criteria was appropriate for determining her choices?

Almost before she had finished hearing the question she heard the answer: her wants. She could choose to do whatever she wanted to do, and if she had a number of different wants, she could choose the one which would bring her the greatest joy and satisfaction. For, from the place of the I AM, every want can only be in harmony with human and earth interests. She also realized that these wants could and would be fulfilled. For, unobstructed by ego fears and limited attitudes, Self spontaneously nourishes and satisfies itself, creating for itself the appropriate circumstances for its well-being and continuing unfolding.

As our individual river flows into the ocean of Self, becoming finds its being. And in the being of Self there is authentic freedom. Not the freedom of the psychological adolescent who casts off parental restraints and familial obligations in pursuit of ego independence. For though this "freedom" is an essential part of ego development without which there can be no realization of Self, it is the polar opposite of authentic freedom inasmuch as it is "freedom" from others, from authority, from environmental circumstances rather than the freedom which arises spontaneously from the recognition and experience of the interdependence of human beings, earth, and universe. This freedom alone is the one no person or situation can take away. For it is not a freedom from any thing but the freedom of being at the source of creation, the freedom of being Self. It is complete and eternal, unthreatened by the vicissitudes of life; able to live as fully in the soul of a bonded laborer or an inmate in a concentration camp, as in the hermit in a Himalayan cave. The realization of this freedom enables us to choose our state of being whatever the outer circumstances of our lives.

In his account of life in a German concentration camp, Viktor Frankl writes of those who glimpsed such freedom:

We who lived in concentration camps can remember the men who walked through the huts comforting others, giving away their last piece of bread. They may have been few in number, but they offer sufficient proof that everything can be taken from a man but one thing: the last of the human freedoms—to choose one's attitude in any given set of circumstances, to choose one's own way.

And there were always choices to be made. Every day, every hour offered the opportunity to make a decision, a decision which determined whether you would or would not submit to those powers which threatened to rob you of your very self, your inner freedom; which determined whether or not you would become the playthings of circumstance, renouncing freedom and dignity to become molded into the form of the typical inmate.

Seen from this point of view, the mental reactions of the inmates of a concentration camp must seem more to us than the mere expression of certain physical and sociological conditions. Even though conditions such as lack of sleep, insufficient food and various mental stresses may suggest that the inmates were bound to react in certain ways, in the final analysis it becomes clear that the sort of person the prisoner became was the result of an inner decision, and not the result of camp influences alone. Fundamentally, therefore, any man can, even under such circumstances, decide what shall become of him—mentally and spiritually. He may retain his human dignity even in a concentration camp. Dostoevski said once, "There is only one thing that I dread: not to be worthy of my suffering." These words frequently came to my mind after I became acquainted with those martyrs whose behavior in camp, whose suffering and death, bore witness to the fact that the last inner freedom cannot be lost. It can be said that they were worthy of their sufferings.

(Viktor Frankl, *Man's Search for Meaning*, trans. Ilse Lasch, rev. and enl. ed., Boston, 1970, pp. 65–66)

The capacity to live with dignity and consideration can be acquired in some cases through conscious training, but often such means only succeed by repression of emotional pain, of wounds and desires, without whose acceptance, integration, and healing our souls remain impoverished, less than what they might be and therefore less able to reflect and experience the unity of body and spirit. The dignity and consideration born by such means, though often considerable, tend to be characterized by control and endurance, to lack the serenity, vitality, and playful relaxation which define the freedom born from union with Self.

With the realization of this authentic freedom, choice acquires a significance it did not have while we were traveling into Self. For it becomes the choice not to follow, but to create, the choice to consciously exert the will of I. But after the years of subordinating the will of ego to the greater will of soul—the years of suffering and allowing—such a turnabout is not easy. For to own the freedom of the will, now stripped of its identification with the personal and the ephemeral, means relinquishing the security and safety provided by flowing with the river and consciously assuming responsibility for being a co-creator of our human, earthly, and cosmic realities.

At one level this is nothing new. For at each moment of our being and becoming we are creating this universe. Every thought, feeling, image, and action is in some way forming who we are and the world in which we live. While we operate from an ego perspective, one which inevitably sees life in terms of separation, limitation, conflict, and finite resources, our creation, both in the world and in our own souls and bodies, will reflect such a perspective, giving rise to greed, fear, competition, and jealousy with their inevitable and familiar social and physiological consequences. As we turn and begin to walk into our pain, back to our source, the ego perspective is gradually subordinated to a soul perspective, one which sees life in terms of its own reality—abundant, joyful, interconnected, and capable of expressing its immortal vitality physically, psychologically, and spiritually. As we reach the end of this particular journey and unite with Self, we move into a new age of freedom and co-creation. Our focus is no longer on listening to, following, and serving soul on its journey into Self. For, in uniting with Self, we have stepped into the village of the gods and goddesses, found our place as integral, conscious members of this divine community, and begun to play our part in the creative decisionmaking which is responsible for this and other worlds.

Initially we may be troubled by such questions as "What if I make the wrong creative decision?" until we realize that there is no right or wrong in the place of Self. For by definition the Self cannot do something which harms the essential interests of the whole—the earth and all that it contains. Damage can only occur when we forget, slip out of this union with Self. And this, of course, happens frequently in the early months and years following union with Self. So continual attentiveness is necessary, constant monitoring to see that we are living out of our most joyful place, that the decisions we make are born from serenity, love, peace, and creativity.

Inasmuch as we choose not to diminish ourselves by returning to redundant attachments, to the unnecessary tensions of separateness, but enjoy instead the relaxed warmth and peaceful fulfillment of union with Self, the turbulence of feeling and thinking which characterizes the journey to the ocean spontaneously stills itself. No control is required, merely quiet attentiveness to the flowing universe which we are. And in this stillness we find the freedom and inclination to become gardeners of both earth and soul, delighting in the possibilities of assisting them toward greater degrees of beauty and well-being.

Nature is hungry for this kind of attention, this human relating. For while earth's wildernesses offer vital opportunities for us to awaken to, enjoy, and finally integrate our own wild, instinctive spaces, these raw, untamed regions have needs of their own, needs not served by their remaining wildernesses. For though nature conservation is useful inasmuch as it protects some of this earth from the brutal, exploitative hands of human greed and unrelatedness, it is merely a first step. Conservation serves as a holding operation until there are enough people who, having integrated their own wildness, their own raw instinctuality, no longer need the mountains, deserts, and arctic regions to provide this for them, and can begin to change their relationship to nature from one of taking to one or giving, can begin to assist the unfolding of nature as it, for millennia, has assisted our own unfolding.

Where, even in small ways, human gardening has occurred, not out of a desire to harness nature in the interests of personal or social aggrandisement and control, but out of devotion for nature's possibilities, the earth breathes a warmer and gentler spirit, apparently grateful for the caring attention of the human world.

The attitude of the authentic gardener has a creative contribution to make in other fields—political, social, and economic. He or she can create forms which unfold the highest and deepest possibilities of those whom they are designed to serve. And as with earth gardening, there is no right or wrong form, provided it is conceived and born from the place of Self, but rather many changing possibilities reflecting the changing nature of the people involved. Like nature gardening, social gardening begins with certain raw materials, such as the fact of childbirth and the need for loving education and parenting. But beyond this there are no givens, no musts or oughts to guide the forms in which these needs can best be served. Instead, there is the space for the free play of the imagination born from the unconditional love that is Self.

Fostering the creative imagination, therefore, becomes an exciting and potentially revolutionary act. But, as with all creative acts, it depends on death as well as birth: the conscious surrender and dissolution of old concepts and patterns of thinking and doing, so that new ones, more in tune with the deepest interests, the I AM of the people, may have space to be seen and heard. To imagine new forms of parenting and human relating, for example, requires letting go of old ones, risking the shifting ground as well as containing the emptiness, the waiting receptivity, so as to create a womb in which the new may be conceived and gestate.

Most of our mental concepts are glued in place by our emotional wounds and needs. Yet even after these have been recognized, suffered, and healed, the old ideas and attitudes do not necessarily fall away without our cooperation but need to be consciously relinquished. This mental undressing does not hurt like emotional undressing—the sacrifice of attachments to the ephemeral so that we may be filled by the eternal. The vast terrain of possibility which it opens up not only awakens a profound unknowingness but convinces us of the power of thoughts and our responsibility for wielding this power with love and insight. Opportunities for healing and creation reveal themselves as we gradually learn that each choice in thinking is a creative act with repercussions not only in the imaginative realm but also—provided the thought is sufficiently sustained and warmed by the heart—in the denser plane of matter.

The significance and power of negative thoughts and emotions had first become clear to Sally during the liminal time between the dying and the birth of I AM, when her body was severely depleted by psychological suffering. But it was only much later that she became aware of the power of thought to create or destroy the physical body. It occurred to her by way of a dream during the time in which she was puzzled as to why her physical stamina was not improving even though her heart was now at peace:

In the dream she saw a man who was dying of an AIDS-like collapse of the immune system. All the doctors diagnosed his condition as terminal and disagreed only over the amount of physical life left to him. But one night as he was lying in bed, permeated by thoughts of his own dying, a voice told him that his body would heal if he thought of it as healthy. Following this advice the man filled himself with thoughts and images of health. Instantly his body began to drink in the life of these thoughts, becoming stronger moment by moment. By the end of the dream the man no longer had AIDS and was already moving toward physical health.

This dream reflected the turning point in Sally's physical recovery from the chronic weakness and final collapse of her health brought about by her way through pain. In the early days and weeks following the dream she often found it difficult to maintain the thoughts of well-being when her body was still demonstrably unwell and exhausted. She would find herself assailed by images of death and disease. But each time she chose to exchange such thoughts for ones which better reflected the eternal and unlimited health of Self, she felt her body absorbing new vitality.

The surrender of outworn habits of being, thinking, and doing and the assumption of our power to create our own reality with our thoughts, will, and imagination complete the process of dissolution and dismemberment which characterizes the journey of the river of soul to the illimitable waters of the sea. What begins as an intensely introspective, introverted, and personally absorbed process—years of exploring, analyzing, suffering, and integrating parts of our-selves—leads to the disintegration of the distinction between self and other, between my well-being and yours, or human and earth well-being.

Union with Self unveils the strength to live in the now, shorn of ego-oriented hopes, fantasies, or goals, even by visions of our be-coming. For it provides a serenity and love which lives undisturbed through each moment of the day, whether we are scrubbing the floor, weeding the garden, putting out the trash, or writing a sym-phony.

Such joyful serenity closes the last gate on the era of emotional pain and opens a new gate—one leading to a more interior sanctuary within the temple of Self. For while union with Self completes the journey to the temple, the journey home, it only brings us to the outermost courtyard of this temple. Many more courtyards, still un-known and unseen, lie between this and the inner sanctuary, from whose vantage point this passage appears a brief and relatively insignificant thing.

In her dream Sally saw a grotesque, luminous green creature. She was repelled by it, knowing that there were an unlimited number of similar green creatures all over the world. She was also terrified. For it was clear that these creatures were the source of all evil and disease. If anyone approached them, they opened up and exuded a ghastly scarlet liquid which caused a fatal disease. All over the world people were locking themselves in their rooms, bolting doors and windows, to keep out these creatures. But their efforts were useless, as the creatures, able to assume any shape they wished, could creep through the air cracks under doors and around windows. There was no way of defending oneself from their fatal presence.

Amid this atmosphere of terror and flight, a tall, radiant being of love appeared and asked Sally to walk with him toward the largest green creature. He explained to her that his task was to free the world from these creatures, but that he could only do this with her cooperation. They needed to walk together toward the creatures with their attention singlemindedly focused on love. Any fear, he ex-plained, would strengthen the power of the creatures, since fear was their food.

So he and Sally unlocked the doors and began walking toward the green creature. When they reached it they climbed on its back and rode it like a small animal. Instantly it began to change and shrink and was soon no larger and no more frightening than a small puppy.

Sally knew that this creature and all other ones would now cease to exist, unable to survive in a world imbued by love.